WATCH OUT FOR
HIGH PLACES!

In my dream, I stood on a high cliff over water. Hands dug into my shoulders—hands that meant to kill me. I screamed and stumbled backward. Another shove, and I was at the cliff's edge. "Stop it," I screamed. "Darren!" The hands shoved hard. I tumbled into blackness, toward something that took on form as I hurtled toward it. It was a face, its lips drawn back in a snarl of fury. When I met that face, I would die.

THE DEADLIEST OF FRIENDS

Mary Main

Special thanks to my agent, Kendra Marcus, and to Larry and Ellen Herscher, Sierra campers extraordinaire, for their invaluable assistance.

For Bob,
the most awesome skier on the lake

Chapter *1*

*T*he second our Jeep rolled to a stop in front of the lodge, I threw open my door. "I'm going to check out the lake."

"Hey, slow down, Megan." James shoved his keys in the pocket of his hiking shorts as he climbed out after me. "You're not going anywhere yet."

My brother could be a real pain. Didn't he realize how much I missed the ocean and our beach at home? It was his brilliant idea to come back to Sapphire Lake, where we'd spent the summer with Mom and Dad eight years ago. He thought it would be fun to see the place again, but not me. If there was anything more boring than a bunch of mountains and pine trees, and a body of water with no waves, I couldn't think what. James was a hiker, so for him this was paradise. "You have a smudge on your glasses," I said.

"Don't change the subject." He wiped his horn-rims on the sleeve of his shirt and put them back on. Then he looked down at me. His eyes were the same light green as mine.

"I promised Mom and Dad I'd watch out for you, kid, so listen up. These mountains can be dangerous. Steep cliffs. Freezing cold water. And the altitude will knock you out."

James knew I hated heights and probably expected me to cringe in fear at his warning. "Are you going to spend the rest of the summer lecturing me, big brother?"

"Not if you stay out of trouble." He checked his watch. "It's almost six o'clock. We have to register and get our bags to our rooms before dinner."

I turned and started running toward the lake. "I'll be back in time," I yelled over my shoulder.

"Meg!"

I ran faster. Arguing with my brother was pointless. He never changed his mind. Dad said we'd inherited the Delandry stubbornness along with our eyes, our tall, thin bodies, and our brown hair. Otherwise, we were nothing alike. James was a total brain, like Mom and Dad. My best subjects were lunch and volleyball.

I walked to the end of a nearby dock and plopped down between a Chris Craft and a rowboat. The wooden boards were warm, and the lake was blue and sparkling. The July sun felt good on my legs. Freedom, I thought, as the pine-scented breeze lifted my hair around my shoulders, and I stretched my arms overhead.

A whining noise rose in the distance, and a yellow Bayliner raced over the water. The boat circled the cove, whipping up a spray of white water, and tore back out toward an island in the middle of the lake.

I sat up, shading my eyes. I'd never seen a

Bayliner go that fast. The boat doubled back, aiming directly at me, then slowed in a huge slosh of water. "Megan, is that you?" a guy yelled at me from the driver's seat. His hair shone like a hawk's feathers in the sun.

I smiled and jumped to my feet. I remembered that face. Darren Rourke and James had been buddies during the summer we'd stayed here. Darren had been nice to me, even though I was a kid at the time. I'd had a crush on him, if you could call my seven-year-old awe a crush. "Hi!" I waved.

He folded his arms over the steering wheel. "I heard you were coming. How about a ride?"

I glanced up at the road. James was walking up the path toward the lodge. "Sure," I said.

The engine spit bubbles underwater as Darren guided the boat next to the dock. I climbed over the rail and sank into the passenger seat, folding my legs into the space under the dashboard.

"You've grown up," he said.

"Yeah." I looked up at him. What I saw shocked me like a blast of ice water. Scars. Horrible ones. His left cheek was dark and rippled, as if a truck had run over his face. The purple ridges just missed his eye and ran up his forehead into his hair. I guessed he was trying to smile, but his lip drooped on that side, like a creature in a horror movie.

"Uh, you've grown up, too," I croaked.

His dark blue eyes looked . . . what? Scared? I pressed my lips together to make sure my mouth wasn't hanging open with shock. He turned away.

The right side of his face was fine, with smooth skin, straight nose, and square jaw. He wore a T-shirt and shorts, and his body was tanned and muscular. If it wasn't for the scars, he'd be great-looking. As it was, he didn't look quite human.

He punched the gas, and the boat shot away from the dock. I glanced back at the shore. Maybe this wasn't such a hot idea, I thought to myself.

Darren took the boat to cruising speed. "Everybody wants to know how my face got trashed, so I won't keep you in suspense."

I shoved my hair out of my eyes. "You don't have to talk about it if you don't want to."

"I'm getting used to stares and questions. Little kids are the worst." His voice was low and scratchy, and I had to lean closer to hear him over the sound of the engine. He grabbed a black baseball cap from the shelf under the windshield. "I got burned in an explosion." He jammed the cap onto his head and pulled it down over the left side of his face. "I'm having plastic surgery, but it takes time. They've already done some skin transplants." He looked at me with something between a smile and a sneer. "You probably haven't noticed, but there's more to do."

I cleared my throat. "When did it happen?"

"In May." He turned back to the water. "Are you and your brother here alone this summer?"

May was only a couple of months ago, and I wanted to ask if the burns still hurt. But it didn't take a genius to figure out he wanted to change the subject. Be cool, I told myself. "Yes, we're alone. Mom and Dad are in Russia on an archaeological dig. They'll be back in September. Now that James is in college, they think he can take care of me." I tossed back my hair.

"How old are you now?"

"Fifteen." Darren was a year younger than James, I remembered, so he'd be eighteen now.

"Well, you got lucky staying at the Valaskioff."

"*Valaskioff*." The word felt strange on my tongue. I glanced at the gray stone mansion on the shore. Three stories tall, the stately lodge sat on a knoll under a stand of giant pine trees. Tangled red and blue flowers lined a path leading to the wide porch. "What does the name mean? I can't remember."

"Heaven's Crag." He let out a strangled laugh.

"You don't think it fits?"

"No way." He made a quick turn around a floating log.

"Why not?"

"Because it's more like hell than heaven up here."

"That's a weird thing to say."

"It's a weird place lately. But, hey, you're here on vacation. Let's talk about the good stuff. Wildlife. Water to ski on. Mountains to climb."

"I'm not big on mountain climbing," I said. "What happens around here in the way of social life?"

He shrugged. "I hear Karen's planned something for tonight." Karen Thorsten was the daughter of the Valaskioff's owners.

"Are you going?"

"No." He pulled his cap lower over his face.

"Why not?"

"Not invited."

"Why?"

He jerked the wheel so hard that I bumped my arm on the side of the boat. The bow popped out of the water with a surge of speed that sent us flying. Darren scowled out at the lake, and I couldn't tell if he was angry or just concentrating on his driving. But he sure hadn't wanted to answer my question. Was I being nosy, like James always said?

The wind doused us with spray. Relax and enjoy the ride, I told myself. I held my arms up. The spray stung my skin, and the wind whipped through my hair. The sun was still strong, but the sky was turning pink. A red-tailed hawk circled above us, and I felt like I could soar up to meet it in the air. It was the same bursting feeling I got when my board shot through the waves at Malibu. The speed was addictive. I could never get enough.

We circled the lake, and Darren eased back on the power. I let my hand drop over the side as we drifted slowly toward the dock. The water swished through my fingers like melted ice cubes. "Great ride," I said. "You water ski, don't you?" I vaguely remembered him flying around the lake behind his dad's boat.

"Oh, sure." His eyes were serious. "I ski."

"Would you teach me?"

He looked off into the distance, then at me.

"I'll show you how to ski, but I have to tell you something first. After you know, you might not want to come out with me."

I combed my hair back with my fingers. "I can keep up with you, if that's what you're worried about."

"That's not it. You're going to hear the story, anyway. You might as well hear it from me."

I glanced toward shore. James and a blond girl stood talking on the beach. That has to be Karen, I thought. James turned, waved his arms in the air, and yelled something. "Darren, I'd better get back before my brother has a cow."

"In a minute." Darren's eyes looked darker now, cold and hard as blue marbles. "Do you remember Brad Houston?"

"Sure. The blond kid that played with you and James. He was your best friend, right?"

"Right." He leaned toward me, and I tensed at the closeness of his mangled face. "A few months ago he was driving my Ski Nautique. I was on the dock, waiting to ski. The boat exploded." He rubbed the skin near his eye, as if telling the story caused his face to be burned all over again. "He was killed."

"Brad's dead?" I couldn't breathe.

"There's something else." His face was a dark purple on the one side—angry-looking, like his eyes.

"What?" I whispered.

"No one believes it was an accident. Everyone thinks I murdered Brad."

Chapter 2

I pressed my back into the seat and stared at him. "How did it happen?"

"Brad was careless." He pounded the wheel with his fist. "I warned him to ventilate the engine. Gas fumes . . . I should have done more, should have forced him to be careful. Sometimes the only thing Brad understood was a fist to the jaw."

I hoped he couldn't hear the thudding in my chest.

"We skied together every morning," he went on. "Usually we'd take a run across the lake to see if the water was glassier on the other side." His voice calmed, as if he were telling a story that had happened to someone else. "That morning it was primo water right here, smooth as a mirror, so we decided to ski off the dock. Brad wanted to evaluate my dock start. He told me to go first. I was standing at the end of the dock when he fired up the engine. The boat blew apart." Tears sprang to his eyes. "I swear I didn't do it."

"Did the police investigate?"

"Oh, yeah." He frowned. "But they don't have anything on me."

I nodded slowly.

"You don't believe me, do you." He gunned the engine, and we shot toward shore.

"It's not that—"

"Can't blame you. No one else does, either." He stared at the water as we raced to the end of the dock and pulled alongside. "See you around, Megan."

"Let's talk later." I climbed onto the dock.

He wrenched the wheel, and the Bayliner roared off.

The boards shook under my feet, and I looked up to see James stomping toward me.

"Where have you been, Megan?" he yelled.

I walked slowly toward him. "On a boat. With Darren Rourke. You remember him, don't you?"

He jabbed a finger in the air. "I told you not to be long. Did you expect me to carry your bags in for you?"

"Chill out. I'll carry my own bags."

"Why didn't Darren stick around?"

"Maybe he didn't feel like it." But I wondered myself why he hadn't stayed to say hello to James. Or course, he was upset. And maybe he was sick of explanations. I folded my arms, figuring Karen had told my brother about the boat explosion. Had she also told him Darren did it? "You're not my father, you know, James."

"I'm Dad's substitute for the summer, and don't you forget it."

"If I do, I'm sure you'll remind me."

"Don't go off like that again without telling

me." He whipped off his glasses and wiped them on his shirtsleeve. "Agreed?"

"I'll think about it."

Karen joined us on the dock and held out her hand. "Hi, Megan." Her eyes were light blue, her lashes and brows the same sunbleached-blond as her hair. She wore a bright red T-shirt displaying a white shield with a bow and arrow inside. Her name and that of the lodge, Valaskioff, swept across the bottom in large script. Navy blue hiking shorts completed her outfit.

"I couldn't believe it when James called last spring for reservations," she said. "Voice from the past. It's great to have someone under forty and over ten staying with us."

"Thanks." I shook her hand. Her grip felt like a guy's.

"I'll talk to you later, Meg," James said. "I want to take a bike ride before dinner. Your bags are in the Jeep. You'll be here when I get back?"

"Maybe," I replied none too sweetly.

"Ready to see your room?" Karen ran a hand through her short, blunt-cut hair.

"Ready."

When we got to the Jeep, I grabbed my bags and followed Karen into the lodge. She was a couple of inches shorter than me and had bulging calf muscles. A Swiss army knife protruded from the back pocket of her shorts. She hadn't changed much from the stocky kid who'd been the best fort builder on the beach.

Karen reminded me that the Valaskioff had

been built to look like a castle from Norse mythology. Downstairs there was a huge dining room, a rec room, and a library. The library held a giant padlocked cabinet filled with rifles. "Father's collection," Karen said when I asked her. "I hunt with a bow and arrow," she added. "It's a lot more sporting." I nodded as we climbed the stairs past two wooden landings to the third floor.

"The smaller rooms are in this wing." Karen waved at the hallway of wooden doors, each one displaying a scene carved into the wood. "I'm up here, too. Right over there." She pointed to a door with a fierce-looking woman holding a bow and arrow in one hand and a shield in the other. "Norse warrior goddess. Looks just like me, huh?" She gave a loud laugh and marched ahead of me.

"Is that where you got the idea for your T-shirt?" I asked.

"What? Oh, yeah." She pointed to another door. "Here's your room, the one with the bighorn sheep on the door. Sorry we couldn't get you next to James. He's in the bluejay room down the hall."

I grinned. "I'll try to survive."

"If you need anything, holler. We can catch up on things tonight. Right now, I've got to help Mother with dinner. We eat at seven."

"Just one question," I said. "Is Taffy still here? Or maybe one of her kittens?"

Karen frowned. "We don't have cats anymore. Father decided he didn't want them around."

"Really? But Taffy had been your pet for a while, hadn't she?"

"Yeah." She turned abruptly and walked down the hall. Soon she was out of sight.

My room had a four-poster bed and braided rug with balloon shades at the windows. Over the desk, a print of a knight in a horned helmet glared at me. Above the shades, a strip of stained glass filtered red light into the room. No fireplace, but the view was terrific.

I tossed my bags onto the red-and-white bedspread and walked to the window. Out on the lake, Darren's Bayliner flashed yellow on the dark blue water. His dad's speedboat, I remembered, had been yellow, too. Mr. Rourke had driven Darren and Brad over here many times to play with James.

That had been my cat phase, and every morning after breakfast I'd sat on the porch, playing with Taffy. One morning when I couldn't find her, I'd panicked, picturing her wandering in the forest, being stalked by wild animals. By the time Darren's dad dropped the boys off, I was crying. Brad ran past me to find James, but Darren stopped and bent down. "What's wrong?" he asked.

"Taffy's run away," I sobbed. "She's lost."

"Hey. Come on." He took my hand and led me down the steps. Then he tapped his fingers on the bottom of the house. "Here, Taf. Come on, girl."

Before long, the cat's golden head appeared

through a hole in the concrete. She slunk out, purring, and rubbed against Darren. "See?" he said. "Sometimes she hides under there to get away from people. Not a bad idea, huh?" He then dropped Taffy in my arms and took off. After that, I'd talk to Darren whenever I could. He even taught me to whistle through my fist, like the guys did. I've fooled James a couple of times with that whistle.

Back home in Santa Monica, I sent him a couple of letters with pictures I'd drawn of the lake and dumb notes like, "I liked rafting on Sapphire Lake" and "Thanks for teaching me the whistle." Once he sent me his class picture, which I saved until it finally disappeared somewhere in my desk.

I grabbed a brush and pulled it through my tangled hair, thinking back to our conversation in the boat. Darren was different now, kind of sad and scowly, but that wasn't surprising when you knew what was going on in his life. Had he killed Brad? It almost seemed like he could have, the way he was acting—so defensive and all. I dropped the brush on the bureau, unzipped my duffel bag, and started unpacking.

We ate dinner with the rest of the lodgers, about twenty people made up of little kids, parents, and senior citizens. Afterward Karen led James and me out to the dock and revved up the Chris Craft.

"Where are we going?" I sat down on the damp seat next to James.

"Moon Island." She steered away from the dock.

"What for?"

"To meet someone."

"Who? Someone we used to know, like Roberto?"

"No, he's babysitting his little brothers tonight. His parents worked out a point system where he's earning a car for taking care of the kids."

"Who is it, then?"

James laughed. "Megan the Nose."

"Shut up." I punched him on the arm.

"I want you to be surprised," Karen said.

I stared curiously at the island as we sped toward it. I'd been there a few times with Dad, but I'd been too young to explore it on my own.

Ten minutes later we beached the boat. The sand and hillside glowed in the pale yellow moonlight. Somewhere a dog barked, and the noise echoed like a stone skipping across the lake.

"Let's go." Karen stepped onto a narrow path leading up to a high cliff, and James followed.

"You mean we're going to hike up there?" I groaned.

"Come on, Meg," James said. "It'll be character-building."

"You know I hate this stuff," I muttered. But I dug my feet into the rough, steep ground and pushed to keep up with them.

Before long, James took off on his own, moving quickly ahead of us.

"Hey, Karen . . ." My foot scraped the ground, and pebbles clunked down the path behind me. My stomach bolted, and I didn't dare look down.

"Yeah?" She turned slightly.

"You and Darren are friends, aren't you?"

"No!" She stopped and glared at me. "I hate the creep!"

I tripped over a clump of roots, and it took a second to catch my breath. "Why?"

"Because Brad's dead, and it's his fault."

"Do you really believe that?"

"I wouldn't say it if I didn't. But now's not the time to talk about it."

"All right." I was too out of breath to talk, anyway—thanks to the altitude.

At the top of the cliff, I took deep breaths while Karen walked ahead. Finally my wind came back. I pulled off my sweatshirt and tied it around my hips. The lake swayed a hundred feet below, and as I looked at it, an ugly image came into my mind—the Ski Nautique exploding in a fireball, killing Brad and burning Darren's face. Had it really been murder? And if Darren hadn't done it, who had?

Chapter 3

$\mathcal{I}$ backed away from the edge. Above me, stars were smeared across the inky blue sky. The trees stood dark and majestic on the far mountainside, and I wondered about the secrets they guarded.

"Pick it up, Megan," Karen called, and I turned and jogged toward her.

"We got lucky." She pointed to a soaring mountain in the distance. "You can see the peak of Devil's Tail tonight. It's usually hidden by clouds."

"I'm going to climb that mountain this summer." James folded his arms and stared out at it.

"Not without a guide, you aren't." Karen crunched toward him over thick pine needles. "There are no trails, and it's risky climbing above 10,000 feet."

"The lodge provides a guide, doesn't it?"

"Yeah." Karen nodded. "Me."

"Then let's set up a time."

"It's not my favorite hike," Karen said, looking off into the distance.

"Then I'll go alone," James told her. "I can handle it."

"Not while you're staying with us and we're

responsible," Karen replied. "If it's that important to you, I'll take you up."

"Good!" James turned to me. "You should come, too, Meg. The only way to get over your fear is to face it head on."

"Thank you, Dr. Shrink," I said. The mountain did look like a Devil's Tail, with its thin peak and triangle-shaped top. One flick of that tail and a person would go hurtling through space to a crushing death on the rocks below. I shivered at the thought.

Karen led us into a small meadow surrounded by pines. At the far edge, where the cliff gave way, a girl dressed in white stood staring out at the water.

"Julie," Karen called. "We're here."

The girl slowly turned around.

"Oh, hello," she said in a whispery voice. "Megan and James, right? Karen told me you were coming." She raised one arm toward the sky. "Isn't it a beautiful night?" A lavender jewel glittered at her throat, an amethyst, I guessed.

"Sure is." James pushed up the sleeves of his shirt and grinned at her.

"Do you live up here?" I asked.

She laughed softly. "No. I live in the big brick house near the lodge. We moved in a couple of years ago." She turned to Karen. "Where's Roberto?"

"With his brothers." Karen made a face. "Glad I don't have any brothers or sisters to worry about. You ready for us, Julie?"

"Yes." Julie hugged herself and looked up at the darkening sky. "I'm so happy you asked me to do this, Karen. I love reading the future. Especially for people I've never met before."

I stepped toward her. "You mean you're going to make predictions about us?"

She nodded. Her earrings flashed lavender under her pinkish red hair.

James shoved his glasses up on his nose. "Fortune-telling? What a crock."

"James is famous for his open-minded attitude," I said.

"Fortune-telling is a rather old-fashioned term," Julie explained. "I tune in to the energy waves that show me what is coming in a person's life."

Karen shoved her hands into her back pockets. "Julie sees things you wouldn't believe."

"You're right. I wouldn't believe it," James said. "How do you interpret these so-called energy waves? With a crystal ball? Or tea leaves?"

I rolled my eyes. "Be rude, why don't you, James?"

But Julie only smiled. I wondered if she dyed her hair to get it that odd color.

"I use crystals, James. My grandmother gave them to me when I was little." She glided toward us, sliding a satin bag from her shoulder. Her white blouse gently billowed out around her as she moved.

"Julie's grandmother was a fortune-teller," Karen told us. "She left the crystals to Julie in her will."

"Cool," I said.

"A bag full of rocks?" James groaned. "This is even loonier than I thought."

"No, this is real and true. The universe is ready and willing to give me answers to the questions I ask. It speaks to me through my crystals," Julie said.

James snorted softly but didn't say anything more.

Julie reached into the bag and pulled out a strip of velvet. She lowered herself gently to the ground, crossed her legs under her white skirt, and shook out the cloth. "Come on. Sit close to me."

We sat down in front of her, the squawgrass parting around us. Her perfume smelled sweet, like bubble gum.

Julie folded her hands in her lap and gazed at me. Her eyes were as pale as a cat's under thick red lashes and eyebrows. And there were little lines at the corners, even though I figured she was Karen's age—sixteen.

"Shall I tap in to your future first, Megan?"

"Sure," I said. But I hesitated before moving closer. Dad had talked about this kind of stuff—fortune-telling, tapping in to the universe, whatever you wanted to call it. *Divination* was what Dad called it. He'd lectured us on ancient cultures that had messed around with the occult. He'd gotten real serious, like he used to when we were little and he'd given us the "don't talk to strangers" lecture. "It's an open invitation to the spirit world," he'd said. "And not necessarily to friendly spirits." But as the crystals spilled from

Julie's bag, I put aside his warning. They were so pretty. And secretly I agreed with James. It wasn't real, so what could happen?

"Have you ever seen anything so wonderful? Every time I see them it's like the first time." Julie sat back to admire the stones. "Choose a handful and arrange them on the velvet, Megan."

I scooped up a mound of crystals and gently tossed them onto another section of the cloth. Wow, I thought. They looked like jewels in a store window.

Julie studied the stones, then looked up at me with her pale eyes. "The quartz crystal tells me you have strength and energy, Megan. You go after the things you want, and they come to you."

I smiled. "That's true. I made varsity volleyball when I was only a freshman."

"If only she'd focus that energy on her school-work," James said, "she might go somewhere in life."

"The only place I want to go is the beach, big brother."

"You chose a tiger's eye," Julie said softly. "Touch it. Feel its energy."

I touched the cool stone. "I don't feel anything."

"Be patient," Julie said. "The tiger's eye is a helper. It helps you reach inside yourself, take the power that's there and use it. There's divine energy inside each one of us, Megan. All you have to do is tap in to it."

I smiled. "Uh, huh."

"Isn't that so?" Julie turned to Karen.

Karen nodded hard. "That's right."

"Megan, what you want most in the world is your freedom," Julie said. "The tiger's eye predicts that you *will* be free—and soon."

I shot James a grin. "Hear that?"

"But I see a warning, too." Julie glanced up suddenly, and her pale eyes held a look I couldn't interpret. "Right here." She pointed at the middle of the cloth. "Two iron pyrite stones. Fool's gold. There's someone in your life who pretends to be your friend. But that person will try to hurt you. Maybe even take your life. You're in danger, Megan."

"Oh, come on." I pushed back from the cloth.

"No, it's true." Karen rocked forward to stare at the crystals. "Whatever Julie sees, it's true. Believe me. She knows things."

"Shall I go on?" Julie's hand reached out toward me.

I backed away from her. I don't believe this stuff, do I? I asked myself.

She touched my hand with her cool, dry fingertips. "Well, Megan, shall I tell you more?"

A crunching sound came from behind us.

"Another time," I said.

Julie glanced up, and her eyes grew wide. I turned around.

Darren was stalking across the clearing. His fists were clenched, his eyes hard and focused. He stomped over to the velvet cloth, bent over, and with a sweep of his arm hurled the crystals into the night.

Chapter 4

"*D*arren!" I leaped to my feet.

His eyes glittered in the dim light. The baseball cap hid most of his scars. "It's her fault." He shook a fist at Julie. "All of it."

Julie patted the ground. "My crystals!"

Karen darted between them. "Throwing the stones isn't going to change things, you jerk," she yelled at Darren. "It's not Julie's fault that Brad's dead."

"My crystals!" Julie groped around in the grass and scooped the stones she was able to find into her bag. She looked up at Darren. "Brad has gone on to another life. Is that why you hate the crystals, Darren? Because they knew he would be murdered?"

He quickly backed away from her. "Brad's death was an accident!"

"Says who?" Karen yelled.

"It's the truth," he said.

"Liar!" Karen spat out the word. "You killed him."

"No, I didn't!" Darren pounded his fist into his palm. "Why would I kill my best friend?"

"You were jealous of Brad." Karen took a step

toward him. "He got everything you wanted, and you know it."

"Wait a minute!" I stepped forward.

"Whoa, kid." I felt James's hands on my shoulders. "Mind your own business for once."

"The truth can't stay hidden forever," Julie said as she rose and stared into Darren's eyes.

Darren wasn't that tall, but he was dark and fierce, and Julie looked like a glass doll standing next to him. He raised his fist, and I thought for a moment that he was going to hit her. Instead he jerked away and marched off into the darkness.

"Stay away from my sister," James yelled after him.

"Oh, James," I sighed. "You geek."

James grabbed my arm to stop me from following Darren. "Rourke's got a real problem."

I tried to yank my arm away. "Yeah, he does. His friends think he's a murderer."

My brother was wiry but as strong as a bear. "Megan always sticks up for the underdog."

"He used to be your friend, too, James." I pulled away.

"Oh, yeah. Darren's a great friend," Karen said.

I turned to her. "What's the story? You were really hard on him."

She folded her arms and stared at me. "He took Brad away from me!"

"What happened?" I asked.

"Come here, James. Sit next to me," Julie called. The sleeve of her blouse fluttered over my brother's arm as they lowered themselves to the ground.

I moved closer to Karen. "Tell me about it."

She gave me a look as we sat facing James and Julie, a look that said she didn't like my questions. But I wasn't going to back off. "Come on. What gives?"

James was listening, too.

Karen scooped up a pinecone and picked at it. "It's no big secret," she said. "Back in April, a movie company came up to Lake Tahoe. They needed boat drivers and water skiers, and Darren talked Brad into doing it with him. He even conned the high school into letting them arrange their classes around work. They were seniors and didn't have much to do, anyway. When the director found out that Darren knew how to do special effects, he was stoked. I went out to the location a few times with Brad. They did radical stuff."

"Like what?"

"Crashes, bombs. It was a cop movie. Right before they were due to finish, one of the actors got sick. They needed a replacement right away. The director offered the part to Brad." She tossed the pinecone. It hit a tree trunk with a small crack. "Darren's always wanted to be an actor, but Brad beat him out on that, like he did with so many things they tried. Darren's got a nasty temper, and he finally lost it."

"The pain he caused will come back to him," Julie said, touching Karen's shoulder. "If not now, then in another life."

Karen looked at Julie. "He should pay for what he did. In this life."

"What if he didn't do it?" I asked. "What if he's telling the truth?"

"Not a chance," Karen said. "Darren can fool people with that angry self-pity act. Don't fall for it, Megan. I know what he can do when things don't go his way."

"Like what?"

"We don't have all night or I'd tell you. Take my word for it—he can get crazy. Ask Roberto. He'll tell you."

"I will." Was it possible he'd changed so much from the friendly kid I'd known?

"James . . ." Julie dumped her stones onto the velvet and looked up at my brother. "You're planning to be a lawyer, aren't you?"

He smiled. "Did your pet rocks tell you that?"

Julie shook her head slowly. Her eyes gazed into his. "I knew you once. In another life."

James took off his glasses and wiped them on his khaki shorts. "I don't know about other lives, but you're right about me wanting to be a lawyer. And you do look familiar."

She touched his arm. "What do you think about Brad's death?"

He slipped his glasses back on. "Karen's story does make you think, but if the police didn't find any evidence, Darren shouldn't be arrested."

"That's for sure," I said.

Karen let out a laugh. "Evidence, shmevidence. He's as guilty as a coyote with a squirrel in its mouth."

"James understands the law, but he doesn't

know that facts are only part of the truth." Julie touched his hand. "Would you like to hear about your future now?"

He looked at her like a seagull checking out a fat shrimp. "Why not?"

"What?" I made a face at him. "You're going to let her tell your *fortune*?"

"Sure," he said, as if there was never any doubt about it. "I'll let the universe talk to me." He scooped up several stones and dumped them on the cloth.

Julie studied them. When she looked up, her eyes were shining. "So many red jaspers . . . The crystals tell me you have great passion, James. You have always been a perfectionist, so demanding of yourself and others. So serious and hardworking. Your spirit body has preserved many conflicts from past lives, but don't worry. You can be healed through guided imagery. I will help you see that we are all part of a higher consciousness." She reached up and touched his cheek. "Look inside yourself, James, and find love."

I'd never seen such a goofy look on my brother's face.

"Great passion?" I groaned.

He waved a hand at me as if to swat away a fly. "I'm a passionate guy."

"About what? Your law books?"

Julie reached for his hands, leaned forward, and whispered in his ear. He smiled and nodded. For a minute I thought he was going to kiss her.

I turned to Karen. "When does she hop on her

broomstick and fly off over the mountains?"

Karen looked at me like I'd turned into a vampire. "Don't say that. Julie's powers are nothing to joke about."

I shook my head. Karen seemed like the last person who would go for this junk. I yanked my sweatshirt off my waist and pulled it over my head. "Let's go, okay?"

Karen got to her feet. "Megan's right. It's time to go. I've gotta get the greenhorns up at the crack of dawn to fish for trout. Need a ride home, Julie?"

"You know I don't," she said.

"Okay." Karen backed away from the clearing. "Come on, Delandrys."

"Hey, Karen, who are you calling a greenhorn?" James got to his feet.

"Who do you think? The people back at the lodge."

He grinned and turned to Julie. "Good night," he said almost shyly.

"Good night." Julie stood and gazed at him. "Remember, James, the only sin is not recognizing your own perfection."

I hung back as James followed Karen across the clearing. For a second, I thought I felt heat on my skin from Julie's eyes. "Do you really believe those rocks can tell the future?" I asked.

"Oh, yes." She smiled. "But only to those who are in tune spiritually." She reached out and caught my wrist in her fingers. I had a sudden image of snakes wrapping around my arm and jerked my hand away.

The cold smile on her face gave me the shivers. "One last thing, Megan. Stay away from high places."

"Why?"

She slowly shook her head. "There isn't anything more I can tell you. Except, after tonight, you will be free."

"Yeah, sure." I turned and hurried away, trying to catch up with James and Karen at the edge of the hill.

"Crystals . . . crystals . . ." I looked back once, but the clearing was empty. Was Julie chanting, or was it the wind in the pines?

We half-slid, half-hiked down the path. A long howl came from above us, followed by several shrill barks. "What's that?"

"Only a coyote, little sister." James nudged me, and I moved faster.

As we climbed into the Chris Craft and sped across the lake, I stared hard at the water, but Darren's Bayliner wasn't around. The dock in front of his house was empty. I wondered where he'd gone and what he was doing.

Back at the lodge, I said good night to James and Karen and climbed the stairs to my room. It had been a long day. I dropped my clothes onto the floor, slipped into bed, and fell asleep.

Chapter 5

*I*n my dream, I stood on a high cliff over water. Hands dug into my shoulders—hands that meant to kill me. I screamed and stumbled backward. Another shove, and I was at the cliff's edge. "Stop it," I screamed. "Darren!" The hands shoved hard. I tumbled into blackness, toward something that took on form as I hurtled toward it. It was a face, its lips drawn back in a snarl of fury. When I met that face, I would die.

I woke up suddenly, my mouth open in a quiet scream. I breathed hard. My forehead felt cold and damp. It's only a bad dream, I told myself. Nothing to be afraid of. But my heart ticked faster than the clock on the table. My teeth ground against each other. I'd had this nightmare before, a long time ago. When was it? I groped for the memory, but it disappeared like a pebble in deep water. Had it been Darren's hands on my shoulders pushing me down?

The clock read 2:13. The moon shone through the colored glass over the window, lighting the bedspread with a red glow. I reached for my sweatshirt, tugged it around my shoulders, and walked to the window. Raising the shade, I looked out on the dark, shimmering water below.

Halfway between the island and the shore, a canoe glided toward the dock. Why was anyone out on the lake at this time of night?

I watched the person tie up and walk up the porch steps into the lodge. It was James! I moved quickly to my door and turned the knob. It wouldn't move. I wrenched it, trying to force it around. Nothing. I yanked it. I rattled it. The knob wouldn't budge. It was either jammed—or locked from the outside. I felt a scream rise in my throat. Was I stuck in here? Footsteps passed in the hall, and I heard a door close. I tried the knob again. It turned easily. Shocked, I stared down at my hand.

In the hall, high sconces made shadows on the stone walls. A crack of light came from under my brother's door. I headed for his room, but a sudden noise stopped me. Someone crying. I hesitated, then turned around and tiptoed in the direction of the sobs. I stopped at the door with the woman carved into the wood. "Karen?" I called softly. The cries stopped.

The woman on the door looked ready to attack me with her bow and arrow. I knocked. "Are you all right, Karen?"

There was a long silence, then the door slowly opened. Karen stood there, dressed in a nightshirt with the same design as on the T-shirt she'd worn earlier, her hair sticking out, her eyes wet with tears. "I'm okay," she said.

"Did you have a bad dream?"

She squeezed her eyes closed and took a

deep, shuddering breath. "I just miss him so much. Nothing's the same. Nothing. He was always there for me. Until it ended. We had so many plans."

"Oh, Karen." I didn't know what to say. No one close to me had ever died. "It must be really awful for you. Would you like to talk for a while?"

She shook her head and ran a hand through her hair. "I've got to get some sleep or I'll be a zombie tomorrow. But thanks for checking."

I gave her what I hoped was a reassuring smile. "Sleep well, then."

"Yeah." She closed the door.

I sighed, turned, and walked back down the hall. The lights were off in James's room. I decided not to bother him. We could talk tomorrow.

When I came down for breakfast the next morning, the dining room was empty. In the kitchen, Karen's mother and another woman were cleaning up. Mrs. Thorsten stood at the sink, rinsing dishes and slipping them into the dishwasher. Sunlight streamed through high windows onto the blue tiled counters.

Mrs. Thorsten looked like an older version of Karen. She wore jeans and a ruffled blouse, and her cheeks were red from the steamy water. "Good morning, dear. There are muffins, quiche, and fresh fruit on the table by the window."

"Thanks," I said, helping myself to a muffin. "Where is everyone?"

"Well, let's see. The Sparling family took a hike to the falls . . . Oh, you mean the young people, don't you? Karen took a group fishing in Desolation Valley. You weren't planning to go with them, were you? They left before I rose at six, and you'd need an experienced guide to get there."

"Now I remember. She and James talked about the fishing trip last night. I'm on my way to the beach. Don't worry about me."

She smiled. "We want you to have a good time, dear. Your parents are such lovely people. We're honored to be entrusted with your care this summer." She held a blue-and-white bowl under the water and slipped it into the dishwasher.

"Thank you, Mrs. Thorsten. By the way, I tried my door last night and couldn't get it open. The doorknob was jammed."

She wiped her hands on a dish towel. "That happens off and on. My husband insisted on modeling this place after a Norse fortress, right down to the locks on the outsides of the doors. Yours might have locked accidentally when you pulled your door closed."

"Maybe Mr. Thorsten could check it and make sure it isn't broken?"

"What . . . ?" Her face turned pale and she leaned against the counter.

"Mrs. Thorsten? Are you all right?"

"Yes . . . It's just that you took me by surprise, mentioning Stefan like that. . . . Didn't Karen tell you?" She took a deep breath. "My husband died earlier this year, on Devil's Tail Peak. He was on a narrow ledge and fell to his death." Her voice broke.

"Oh, no." I felt cold all over. "How awful for both of you."

"Yes. Karen and Stefan were very close. He taught her all about the mountains. Hiking, fishing, boating . . . They did everything together."

"I don't remember him very well. I guess that's why I didn't think to ask about him last night. I'm so sorry."

"You couldn't have known." Her blue eyes filled with tears. I felt terrible that I'd upset her. "Run along, now, dear. It's a beautiful day, and you're here to have fun."

"Thanks, Mrs. Thorsten." I walked outside onto the porch. Poor Karen. No wonder she cried herself to sleep at night. She'd not only lost Brad but her father, too. Darren was right about Sapphire Lake. It was a long way from heaven with all these fatal accidents happening.

Suddenly I remembered my dream. I'd had a similar dream here when I was seven. I was sure of it. Being here again had probably triggered it in my subconscious. Or maybe it was what Julie had said last night—"Stay away from high places." I looked out at the lake, bright blue in the morning sunshine, and I didn't want to think about Julie or her predictions.

A bolt of yellow flared against the water, and engine noise buzzed into the air. There was something else I didn't want to think about. I'd screamed out Darren's name in my nightmare.

I wasn't going to let some stupid dream scare me, I decided. I ran down to the beach and onto the dock, waving my arms. Darren sped toward me. I held my fist to my lips and blew. Shrill and loud.

Darren pulled alongside, and it was the first time I'd seen him laugh. "You are awesome," he said. "That whistle drowned out my engine."

I smiled. "How about a skiing lesson?"

"Sure." He held out a hand and I took it, stepping down next to him. He wasn't wearing his cap, and the sun highlighted every dark purple ridge on his cheek.

We were quiet as we raced across the lake, past the island to the small beach on the opposite shore. Darren eased off the gas, and the boat settled into a rocking motion against the sand. The sun burned down on us, and I studied him. He looked a lot more relaxed this morning.

"This is a good time to ski," he said. "The water's glassy, but it may not last. The wind usually comes up by noon."

"Shall I take you for a run first?"

He looked at me as if I were speaking Russian.

I flipped my hair over my shoulders. "I can drive a boat, you know."

"No." The scowl was back. "I haven't skied since Brad died."

"Oh." I bit my lip. "Sorry."

"Forget it," he said. "You ready?"

"Any time." I peeled off my T-shirt and shorts. I'd worn my bathing suit, knowing I'd be in the water this morning, skiing or not.

"You sure about this?" he asked.

I wasn't sure about anything, but I couldn't let him know that. "Let's do it."

He nodded. "You'd better wear my wetsuit. This water's frigid."

"I'm not planning to be in it that much."

He smiled. "We'll see."

Onshore, Darren helped me fasten on his skis, which he always kept in the boat, and showed me how to hold my body in the water. "Let the boat do the work. Relax, lean back, and keep your knees bent." He moved behind me and rested his hands on my shoulders to steady me. I almost pulled away, remembering the dream, but his hands were gentle.

As I put on my life jacket, he slogged through the water to the boat. Once behind the wheel, he eased away from shore. When the towrope was taut, I gave him the thumbs-up sign, and a great surge of speed dragged me through the water. I got up for about two seconds before I crashed and burned. My second try was better. The third time, I popped out of the water and skimmed over the surface, whoops coming out of my mouth. It was so awesome to be flying over the lake. "Faster. Faster," I screamed.

We circled several times, and I wanted more. Darren handled the boat like a pro. I skied until my arms felt stiff and sore. Finally I tossed the towrope in the air and glided across the water, holding my arms out like wings until I sank into the lake.

As the Bayliner sped toward me, a horrible

picture came into my mind—the boat exploding in a fireball. I closed my eyes, letting my life jacket keep me afloat until Darren picked me up.

Back in the boat, wrapped in a towel, I couldn't stop shivering.

"Told you the water was cold," he said.

"Told you I wouldn't be in it that much."

He grinned. "You don't lie."

"Do you?"

He looked at me hard. "No, Megan. I don't lie." He pulled in the towrope, coiling it around his arm. "Listen, Karen's freaked out over Brad's death. I am, too, so I can sympathize with that. But she's wrong about me."

"She's going to the police. She told James and me on the way home last night."

"She already went. But the police don't have anything."

"If she badgers them long enough, they'll listen."

He shrugged. "There's nothing I can do about it."

"Yes there is."

"What?"

A pair of ducks paddled nearby, the sun lighting their feathers to fluorescent green. "Why don't you find out why Brad was so careless when he knew he could die that way."

"You mean . . .?" He stowed the rope and sat facing me. "Brad would never do anything like that on purpose."

"How do you know that?"

"He had everything. He was happy. You heard Karen. He even got the part in the movie."

"The one you wanted?"

"That's right. Ever since I can remember, I've wanted to be an actor. When Brad got that part, it bummed me out—but I wouldn't blow him up for it."

"Do you still want to be an actor?"

"I don't know. There aren't many jobs around for freaks." He waved a hand at his face. "My parents want me in college. I got accepted at Cal Poly, but I'll have to see how the plastic surgery goes."

I sighed and brushed a strand of wet hair off my cheek. "What did you mean last night when you said all the trouble started with Julie's crystals?"

He leaped up and pounded the back of the seat with his fists. "Those damned crystals!"

I held still, trying not to look shocked.

"She thinks she's some kind of psychic." He turned to me with a scowl on his face. "Right before Brad died, she called us together for one of her sessions. She said Brad was in danger, that he was going to die before the month ended. I thought it was a joke, but Brad got scared."

My heart did a flip-flop. In danger. That's what she said about me. "What did he do?"

"Laughed it off, but I could tell it got to him."

Was it getting to me, too? No, I told myself. The power of suggestion could scare you if you let it. But what about the dream? Hands on my shoulders. Falling. And that ugly face waiting to devour me. That's all it was, I told myself—a bad dream. "Where did you go last night, after you left us?"

"Cruising."

"I didn't see your boat when we left."

"I was probably on the other side of the island."

"Hey, Darren," a voice called.

Surprised, I turned toward the stern. A dark-skinned boy sloshed out of the water and climbed up the boat ladder.

"Roberto! Hi!" I stood and held out my hand to him. "Remember me?" We'd raced each other on our surf mats a few times that summer eight years ago. He was my age and a dynamo in the water. I don't know why I had kept wanting to race him when he cremated me every time.

He stepped into the boat and took my hand in a wet squeeze. "Sure. How you doing, Megan?" Water streamed off his copper skin and shoulder-length, dark hair. He was exactly my height, with lean arms and legs and a hard-looking chest. His deep brown eyes looked past me to Darren.

"Roberto!" Darren got to his feet. "Where did you swim in from?"

"Oh, you know, man. Anywhere. Everywhere." His voice was clear and medium-deep. He nodded at me. "I'm glad you're here. Let's swim together some time."

"By together, you mean me hanging on to your ankles?"

He laughed quietly. "I wanted to come over last night to say hi, but I had to take care of the kids."

"I heard."

"What are you doing here, Roberto?" Darren asked.

"I came to tell you something." He glanced at me, then back to Darren.

"Go ahead," Darren said. "Megan knows what's going on."

Roberto swept back his long hair with both hands. "I have to go to the cops and tell them what I saw the day Brad died. I hate to do it, man, but Karen convinced me to go."

Chapter 6

"*W*hat are you talking about?" Darren shook a clenched fist at him

"That morning. I was there. When the boat blew up."

"Where?" Darren shouted. "I didn't see you."

Roberto backed toward the rail. "Swimming. You guys were busy The Ski Nautique took off from the dock, drifting, you know, and Brad was throwing you the towline. I had to swim around the boat. I remember because I was ticked off that morning about motorboats messing up the lake with gas and oil and noise. Brad turned on the ventilator. I heard it clear as anything. I had time to swim all the way to the Rosemanns' dock before the boat went up. He let that engine air out a long time. It wasn't gas fumes that did it. Not alone, anyway "

Darren glared at him. "You never brought this up before!"

Roberto leaned against the rail as the boat rocked. "I'm telling you now, man. The police think Brad was careless, and that isn't the way it was. Karen's going to drive me into town this afternoon."

Darren pressed his fists against his sides. "Why are you doing this?"

"Nothing personal. I don't want to hurt you, but I can't keep the truth back."

"Yeah, the truth . . . Everybody's version is different."

"Sorry. See you later, okay?" He nodded at me, then dove over the rail and swam to shore with long, easy strokes. I hadn't known him very well when we were here before. He was kind of a loner then, and I wondered if he was still that way.

I turned to Darren. "There's only one truth."

"I didn't kill Brad," Darren said as he sank into the seat facing me. "Roberto's going to get me arrested."

"Not if we find out what really happened."

"I'm beginning to think somebody *did* set that explosion," Darren said.

"But who?"

"I don't know. It was sure strange the way Julie knew in advance that Brad was in danger."

I sat up straight. "Could she be involved?"

He shrugged. "She predicted he'd die. I'd call that a pretty weird coincidence."

"Did she like Brad?"

"Oh, yeah. All the girls did."

"As a friend, or more?"

Darren thought for a minute. "She might have had a crush on him. But Brad and Karen have always been tight, ever since they were kids. Brad was never turned on to Julie as a girlfriend."

"That might've made her mad." I looked out at

the lake. "I remember Brad as a funny kid, always clowning around. Did he have any enemies?"

"Nope." He shook his head. "He was one of those mellow guys. Friends came easily to him, like everything else. You probably remember how I followed him around. Brad was my hero. I wanted to do everything he did. He had looks and brains and, like you said, he was funny. He skied like the wind. Always came in first in competitions. Then he got the part in the movie. As far as I know, only one bad thing ever happened to Brad."

"What was that?"

"Did Karen tell you about her father?"

"Mrs. Thorsten said he died in a fall on Devil's Tail."

"Yeah. Brad's dad was along on that trip with Stefan. He went over the side, too. At that altitude, one false move can be deadly."

I looked up at the sheer mountain behind the lodge. The towering crag seemed to hover over us, but its closeness was an illusion. It was miles away and thousands of feet high. The first time I'd seen it I'd imagined the long fall down, and I shivered thinking about it now. "You're right. The name Heaven's Crag doesn't fit."

"It's like this place has a curse on it or something."

"Maybe it does," I said.

Darren shrugged. "When Brad's dad died, naturally, he was really shook. But he even pulled out of that. He and Karen helped each other through it. Karen's right. I was jealous of everything Brad had, including his relationship with her. They loved each other so much. They lost their fathers, but they had each other."

"Yesterday you said something about Brad only understanding a fist to the jaw." I leaned toward him. "What did you mean?"

He shook his head. "I shouldn't have said that."

"Why did you?"

"I don't know."

I waited, but he wasn't going to say anything more. "How did Brad and Roberto get along?"

He reached for his cap and pulled it on. "Not that well, come to think of it. Roberto was one of the few kids from around here who seemed to like me better than Brad."

"Why did he feel that way?"

"Well, Roberto's what you'd call an eco-nut. He's really into the environment—trees have rights and all that. It used to crack Brad up, and he'd tease the kid—pretty hard sometimes."

"But you took him seriously?"

"I left him alone."

"What about Karen? How did she feel about Roberto?"

Darren smiled. "I know how Roberto felt about her. He was half in love with her, but there was no way she'd give him the time of day. Like I said, she and Brad had been tight since they were toddlers. Anyway, she'd never go for a guy a year younger than her."

"Have things changed between Karen and Roberto since Brad died?"

"You mean does she like him more now? Well, let's put it this way. She knows he's alive. He's been a good friend to her in the last couple of months."

"Who was Brad close to besides you guys? Where did he hang out?"

"We both went to Lakeside High in Tahoe. Otherwise we were stuck here, but Brad never minded. He could be happy spending all day on the lake as long as Karen was around. In winter they snow-skied together."

"Karen doesn't talk much about him, does she?"

He let out a sharp laugh. "She doesn't talk to me about anything. We used to be friends until—"

"Until what?"

"Julie. Karen's really impressed with her. Like Julie has a direct line to the gods or something."

"And Julie doesn't like you?"

He shrugged and half-smiled. "Guess I'm not her type."

"What about Brad's mom? Can we talk to her?"

"She went to San Francisco to stay with relatives after Brad died."

"Then we can't get into the house? To look at his room? Maybe we'll find something there to help us."

He shook his head. "Wait a minute." He turned to me. "Yes we can."

"How?"

"I'll show you when we get there. Let's go to my

place first. I'll make sandwiches, and then we'll check out Brad's room."

"Sounds good. I'm starving."

Cookbooks spilled off the shelves and onto the counters of the Rourkes' knotty-pine kitchen, and I noticed the name Evelyn Rourke on several of them. When I asked, Darren told me that his mother had written them. "That's where I get my awesome talent for cooking," he said as he piled baloney, cheese, and pickles on rye bread. We sat at the round table by the window, devouring the sandwiches.

"I don't remember your parents," I said.

"My dad's a writer, too. They're in New York this month, meeting with their agents. Then they're going up to Cape Cod for a couple of weeks."

"Why didn't you go with them?"

"They didn't ask me. Besides, the police told me not to leave here."

"Oh." I took a bite of my sandwich and chewed. "By the way, you *are* a great cook."

"Yeah, I know."

We talked and laughed, and Darren seemed to let go of his troubles for a while. I was glad to see he could still be fun. Girls were probably crazy about him before the accident. We finished off four minicontainers of chocolate pudding, and then Darren climbed the stairs to his room. When he came back down, we left his house and walked about a quarter of a mile along the lakefront to Brad's place.

The Houstons' stucco house was set back from the lake in a stand of pines. We kicked our way through piles of pine needles to get to the door. Darren took a small metal object out of his back pocket and fiddled with the lock. *Click.* He shoved the object back into his pocket and opened the door.

"What did you do?" I asked. "What is that thing?"

"One of my dad's tools. Brad wouldn't mind," he said.

"Maybe he wouldn't, but is this legal?"

"Like you said, we might find something in Brad's room."

"Right." I glanced over my shoulder. A jay scolded us from a nearby pine tree. No one was around. A loose board creaked as I followed Darren into the house. No turning back now.

Inside, the curtains were closed, the rooms dark. I could hardly breathe in the stale air. I thought about Brad, buried under the earth with no air to breathe. Or had there been enough of him left to bury?

Chapter 7

*B*rad's room was dimly lit, shaded by the surrounding pines. Darren switched on his flashlight and set it on the bureau. Taking a look around, he let out a long, slow breath. "His mom didn't pack up anything, " he said. "It's just the same."

I nodded. Except for the dust, the room looked like someone was still living in it, bed half-made, bike leaning against the wall, ski magazines scattered on the bureau. I stared at a photo of Karen and Brad dressed in prom clothes. Brad had grown up to be a handsome guy, with his blond hair and dark tan; and Karen looked fantastic, her hair waved over one cheek and mascara emphasizing her sky-blue eyes.

"Was Karen really crazy about Brad?" I asked.

"Oh, yeah. Definitely. I wouldn't have been surprised if they'd gotten engaged." His cheeks turned bright red, and he moved so I couldn't see his face.

Had Darren been in love with her, too? She wasn't the type of girl that guys sought out at my school, but maybe up here things were different. She was good-looking enough and could keep up with the guys in anything.

Darren dug into the piles of stuff on Brad's desk. I walked to the bureau, pulled out drawers, and sorted through the contents. Brad hadn't been the most orderly guy. He'd probably saved every gum wrapper since he was ten. We found stacks of clothing and piles of junk but nothing that was helpful.

Darren opened the closet. "Skis, poles, fishing rod . . . that's funny."

"What?"

"Brad's rifle is missing. He always kept it on the closet shelf."

"Maybe his mom took it with her."

"Why would she do that?"

I shrugged. "In case someone like us came poking around where they weren't supposed to be?"

"Good point," he said.

I dug through the stuff on Brad's bureau, feeling guilty for invading his privacy, even if he couldn't care less now. At the bottom of a pile of magazines, I found a crumpled piece of paper with a name and telephone number. "Darren, who's Ron Yarrow?"

He stepped back from the closet. "Yarrow? Never heard of him." He closed the closet door. "If he hung out with Brad, I'd know him."

I showed him the note. "Let's call him."

"Why not?" He reached for the telephone by Brad's bed, then let it drop with a frown. "Dead—of course. We'll have to go back to my place and use the phone."

Back at Darren's house, we walked past the kitchen and climbed the stairs to his room. Over his oak desk, James Dean sneered out at us from a giant poster. Next to that was a Sierra Club poster of a howling wolf. A pair of binoculars sat on Darren's blotter, and next to them a rifle. Not what you usually find on a kid's desk, but, I reminded myself, we were in the Sierras. I ran my fingers over the initials stamped on the Winchester. DLR. I touched the cold steel barrel. Once, I'd asked my mom and dad for a gun and shooting lessons, but they'd looked at me like I'd just announced I was planning to be a drug dealer when I grew up, so I never brought it up again. "Was Brad's rifle like this?"

Darren nodded. "We got them for our birthdays one year. He could drop a deer from three hundred yards." When he shoved his hands in his pockets, with his shoulders hunched, he looked a little like James Dean.

"What about you?" I asked. "Are you a good shot?"

He shrugged. "I can hit a target, but hunting leaves me cold."

"How about teaching me to shoot?"

He looked surprised. "This isn't the best time for that. Maybe someday."

I nodded and glanced at the stacks of books on the table. I picked up a heavy gray textbook. *Firearms and Explosives—Advanced Techniques*, by Kevin Rourke—Darren's father.

"Is this how you learned to do special effects?"

Darren nodded. "Dad confers with the military and the FBI."

"What about picking locks?"

He shrugged. "He knows espionage. That's why his spy novels are big sellers."

I set the book back on his desk.

He turned away. "Let's try that number." He grabbed the telephone, punched in the number, and held the receiver out so I could hear. Five rings, six. No answer. No machine. He dropped the receiver into the cradle.

A sound came from the back of the house. Tires crunching over the rough ground below. Darren moved to the window. "No!" He slammed down a fist on the windowsill.

I looked out. Below us, two police officers stepped out of a patrol car and walked to the back door.

A sharp knock came downstairs. I grabbed the note with Ron Yarrow's number, shoved it into my pocket, and followed Darren downstairs. His steps echoed across the wooden floor as he moved to the door and opened it.

The police officers looked at us. The woman was taller than the man. "Darren Rourke?" Her voice was businesslike.

He nodded.

"We'd like you to come with us, please."

Darren stared at her. "Why?"

"For questioning regarding the death of Bradley J. Houston."

Fear formed a tight knot in my stomach. This

was serious. "Can I go with him?"

She sized me up. "Afraid not."

"Do you want me to call your parents, Darren?" I touched his arm. "Maybe they should come home."

"No! I can handle it."

"But—"

"I said no."

I pressed my lips together, admiring him. If I was in big trouble, I'd want Mom and Dad pronto.

"Let's go, sir," the policeman said.

I followed them outside. Darren got into the backseat of the patrol car. His hair shone darkly inside the back window.

The car bumped up the road, and I watched it until it disappeared into the trees.

Chapter *8*

*J*ays screeched in the forest, and I felt like joining them in their scream-fest. I dodged a tree stump and climbed up a long dirt slope. Was Darren guilty? I couldn't believe it. Or maybe I didn't believe it because I didn't want to. But I was going to find out.

Something whizzed by my ear.

"Watch out!" a voice shouted. "Are you crazy?"

Karen and Roberto stood about ten yards away, holding bows in their hands. To my left, a brightly colored target was propped on a bale of hay.

"Sorry," I yelled. "I didn't see you guys."

"Do you always stroll through target ranges?" Karen threw her shoulders back and stared at me. She looked different from the girl I'd found crying last night. Strong. Together. She let out a mocking laugh.

"Hey, I didn't see you, okay?"

"Well, don't get fumed." Karen lifted her bow. "Ever tried a bow and arrow?"

I shook my head.

"Come on over. Roberto can teach anybody, can't you, Warrior?"

"Hey, don't call me that." He looked embarrassed. "Anyway, you're as good as I am—probably better." He'd changed into jeans and a tank top, and his arms were wiry with muscles. Karen wore her usual red T-shirt.

"I was sorry to hear about your father's accident, Karen," I said.

She turned quickly away. "Julie said it was his karma." Obviously she didn't want to talk about it.

Roberto looked at me and rolled his eyes. "Why don't you just relax and watch us for a while?"

"Sure." I sat on a log, grateful for something to take my mind off Darren at the police station.

The two were expert shots. Eight out of ten arrows whizzed straight to the bull's-eye. I squinted at the target and held out my arm. "Bang," I said under my breath, remembering the handgun at the female officer's waist. I wondered what kind of grades you had to have to get into the police academy.

Roberto let an arrow fly, hitting the bull's-eye once more, then he and Karen walked over to me.

"You guys are good shots." I rose from the log.

Karen smiled. "It's in the genes. Roberto and I come from a long line of marksmen."

I turned to him. "Why did she call you Warrior?"

Roberto set his bow on a flat rock. "Because of my Indian blood."

"What kind of Indian?" I asked.

"Mostly, I'm Mexican, but I have some Paiute. And my grandfather had Washo blood."

"That's why he's such a fanatic about nature," Karen said.

Roberto looked down at the ground. "Yeah. I shoot only at a cloth target, never trees or birds."

"Mr. Purist," Karen said. "That fits you better."

He looked up at her. "It's not a joke, Karen," he said softly. "Look how you're messing up the bark with your arrows." He pointed to a massive pine tree where several nicks marred the rusty red bark.

"Oh, yeah? Well, watch this!" Karen swaggered to the tree, whipped out her Swiss army knife, and carved a design around the marks in the bark. It was a shield, like the one on the door of her room. She turned to us with a mocking smile. "What do you think of that, Mr. Tree-hugger?"

Roberto winced, as if Karen had carved the crest into his skin. Then, with just a hint of a threat in his voice, he said, "Karen, you're going to go too far one of these days."

"Oh, come on. Don't be a wimp." She turned to me. "You know, he can't even stand to hunt? What would your ancestors think about that, Roberto?"

Roberto sighed. "Hunting's an ego thing with you, Karen—that's what I don't like. Like your carving that shield on everything you kill."

She shrugged. "Every hunter needs a mark. My father taught me that."

"Yeah, I know," he said.

"You're deadly serious about ecology, aren't

you?" I asked Roberto, although I could tell just by looking into his eyes that he was.

"Oh, yeah, he is," Karen said. "And it gets stranger."

"What do you mean?"

"The magic. Tell her about that, Roberto."

Roberto pushed back his hair. "Shut up, Karen."

"Oh, Roberto, you're such a bore."

A hurt look flickered across his dark eyes.

"I wish your grandfather were still alive," Karen said. "His stories were dynamite. You never met him, did you, Megan?"

I shook my head. "What kinds of stories did he tell?" I leaned against a pine tree.

Karen shoved her hands into her pockets. "My favorite was the one about a shaman who turned himself into a coyote."

Roberto pulled at his long hair. His fingers were shaking slightly. "This is bad talk, Karen."

"Got the nightmares again?" she asked.

He didn't answer.

I moved closer to Roberto. "You have nightmares?"

"Go ahead, Roberto, tell her." Karen wasn't going to get off his case.

"All right, all right." He turned to me. "I've had a few nightmares, like everyone does."

"What about?"

"He dreams he's riding on an eagle," Karen said. "I think that would be great—zooming through the sky, checking out the scenery."

"That part's good." Roberto squeezed his eyes closed. "The part I hate is when the vultures come. They attack me, and then I know . . ." He turned away.

"What?" I asked. "What do you know?"

"That someone I care about is going down."

"You mean they're going to die?"

"Yeah, die."

I felt cold all of a sudden, even though the sun was penetrating the branches. "Did you have that dream before Brad died?"

"I've been having it for a couple of years."

I thought of my own nightmare. "My mom says dreams can be messages from the angels. Maybe they can also be warnings."

"Could be," Roberto said. "The spirit world can be good, or it can be real bad. I don't fool with it, like our other friend."

"Julie?" I asked.

"She's really tuned in," Karen said. "Were you listening last night, Megan? If I were you I'd be careful who I made friends with."

Karen didn't know that Julie had warned me about high places, but she didn't need to remind me of Julie's other prediction. Both warnings had bothered me all day long. "Does Julie know magic?" I looked at Roberto.

His eyes were so dark that his pupils blended with his irises. "Not Native American magic. Only the old-timers know those tricks."

Psychic stuff seemed to be a hot topic at Sapphire Lake. Even Karen was into it. But

Roberto was right. There were things you shouldn't mess around with. Darren had talked about a curse, but I didn't think that an evil spirit had killed Brad. A living, breathing person had done that.

Karen stared at me, hands on hips. "Speaking of Julie, where's your brother? He was supposed to go fishing with us this morning and never showed up."

"James?" I asked dumbly.

"No, Bigfoot. Yes, James. He hasn't been around all day." She paused. "Roberto and I were at the police station for a while. Maybe we missed him."

"Is that why the police came for Darren?"

Karen smirked. "Yes. And if I were you, I wouldn't be hanging out with a murderer."

I looked at Roberto. "Do you think he killed Brad?"

His dark eyes studied me. "Like I said before, that boat didn't explode by accident."

"But that doesn't prove Darren did it," I insisted.

"He was the only one there besides Brad," Roberto said.

"Except for you," I said.

"That's right." The look in his eyes dared me to accuse him.

"Darren did it," Karen said. "Otherwise he would have been in that boat with Brad. Besides, he was the only one with a reason to be angry with Brad."

She's right, I thought. "What about you, Karen? Where were you when it happened?" I was pushing my luck if I wanted to keep her as a friend, but the question just jumped out of me, as if it had a life of its own.

"Me?" Karen closed her eyes tightly. She was quiet for a long time, and neither Roberto nor I said a word. Somewhere, out on the lake, a calling sound came. A loon? A duck? When Karen spoke, her voice was low. "That day . . . the weather was so great. Sunny. Warm. The first real day of spring. I was painting the rail on the porch."

"That's right," Roberto said. "I saw you and yelled from the Rosemanns' dock. That's when the boat . . ."

"Oh, God." Karen dropped her face into her hands.

Roberto patted her shoulder and turned to me. "Who hired you to play detective around here? Can't you see she's having a tough time?"

"You're right." I turned to Karen. "I'm sorry if I upset you."

"Don't worry about it." She reached for her bow, and I saw tears in her eyes. "How about that archery lesson now?"

"Later, thanks. I think I'll look for James."

"Good luck." Karen smiled. "Julie always gets what she wants, and I think she wants your brother."

I could feel them staring at me as I walked away.

Back at the lodge, I was relieved to see James

sitting on the porch swing, drinking a soda. I flopped into a chair. "When did you get back?"

"A while ago."

"Karen said you didn't show for the fishing trip."

"That's right." He took a long swig of his cola.

"Why not?"

"Something came up."

"What?"

He looked at me over his glasses. "Why are you cross-examining me?"

I grinned. "I've decided to become a cop."

I'd said it to be smart, but once out of my mouth, it didn't seem like such a bad idea. Now he would look shocked and lecture me on getting a Ph.D. if I expected to go anywhere in life. I waited, but he just sipped his soda.

"Seriously, where were you today?" I asked.

"I spent the day with Julie. We had a picnic on the island."

I leaned forward and sniffed. "Whew. Now I can tell. You smell like bubblegum."

He smiled and gazed out at the lake. "She's so great, Meg. It's like I've always known her. We both love the mountains. She said she'd climb Devil's Tail Peak with me."

I grabbed a soda from the ice chest, flipped open the top, and took a long swallow. "Is that where you were in the middle of the night? Messing around with the fortune-teller?"

He straightened up and stopped the swing. "You're too nosy for your own good."

"So you locked my door when you went out?"

"I don't know what you mean."

"I think you do." James had never lied to me before. It gave me a sick feeling in the pit of my stomach to think he might be doing it now. Of course, I hadn't actually heard him unlock the door, and Mrs. Thorsten had said it did get jammed occasionally. "Julie won't make it up Devil's Tail, James."

He moved forward again on the swing, then back and forth. He was making me dizzy. "You'd be surprised how strong she is."

"She must be. She's got you turned on like those crystals of hers."

He smiled.

"James, aren't you going to try to get together with Darren? You guys played together every day when you were kids. He needs a friend right now."

He looked at me without answering.

"Your glasses are smudged," I said.

He waved me off. "I talked to Julie about Darren. She advised me to leave him alone so he could travel his own path to enlightenment."

"Oh, that's brilliant advice."

"I think it is, Meg."

"Well, I don't."

A sudden wind gusted off the lake and whistled through the pines, raining needles down on us. I stared at my brother. He looked at me as if he were seeing me for the first time and wasn't too happy about it. As quick as the wind, something had changed between us, something invisible but so real that goosebumps pebbled my skin. The sun inched toward the horizon, setting the clouds on fire.

"Be careful, James. I think Julie's messing around with something she doesn't understand. Somebody's going to get hurt. Or maybe someone already has."

He frowned at me. "What are you talking about?"

"Dad talked about fortune-telling a few times. Don't you remember? He said it was bad news."

He tapped his soda can with a finger. "You know something, Meg? I think you're jealous. As I remember, you didn't have any qualms about having your fortune told last night. In fact, you accused me of being narrow-minded."

"So I'm not perfect. Big surprise. That doesn't change things. And I'm not jealous!"

James swigged down his soda. "Julie's a special person, so don't put her down. She'd never hurt anyone."

"Do you believe what she said about me being in big danger?"

He looked at me thoughtfully. "I think she's a talented actress, Meg. Not to say that her ideas aren't good. They are. But her predictions are a performance, too."

"Maybe you're right." I took a deep breath. "Are you in love with her?"

He leaned back in the swing, pressing the cola can to his chin. "Feels like it, but I hardly know her. I do know that I've got to play it out, see where it goes."

I sipped my soda. "Want to take a bike ride with me before dinner?"

He looked out at the island. "No, thanks."

"Okay." I stood up and walked into the lodge. I could tell that James hardly even noticed I'd left. A sad feeling suddenly filled me, maybe homesickness, and I couldn't shake it. After tonight, you will be free, Julie had said. Free. Is that what I wanted? I wasn't sure anymore.

I wandered in and out of the rooms downstairs, checking out the Scandinavian artwork. There were a couple of pictures of fierce-looking Vikings and a few of princesses and castles. Several kids watched cartoons in the rec room, and a gray-haired foursome played cards in the living room.

The library was deserted. Two beams carved in the shape of dragons met over the floor-to-ceiling bookshelves, and the room smelled of musty carpets and leather furniture. The rifle case held rows of firearms behind the slightly smudged glass. Next to the case, a deer's head and a mountain lion's head hung side-by-side. I walked up and stared into their cold glass eyes, as if they could tell me what I needed to know. They were silent, dead—like too many others at Sapphire Lake.

I turned away, toward a bulletin board covered by a large map of the mountains. I walked to the door, closed it, and returned to the map. Devil's

Tail jutted above the timberline to eleven thousand feet. That is one big slab of granite, I thought. "A high place for sure," I whispered out loud.

I shoved my hands into my pockets, touching the piece of paper I'd taken from Brad's bureau. Was Ron Yarrow connected to his murder somehow? I walked to a nearby telephone, pulled out the note, and punched in the number. Three rings. Four. I was about to hang up when a man's deep voice came on the line. "Hello."

"Hello," I said. "Is this Ron Yarrow?"

"Yeah, this is Ron. Who's this?" His voice was rumbly.

"I'm a friend of Darren Rourke."

"Don't recognize the name."

"He was a friend of Brad Houston's," I said in a businesslike voice.

"The kid who died in the boating accident?"

"Yes." I twisted the cord around my wrist and paced to the end of the sofa.

"I hated to read that news. Brad seemed like a nice kid. Had everything going for him."

"Then you knew him personally?"

"Not well."

"Can I ask when was the last time you saw him?"

"You say you were a friend of Brad's?"

"Yes." I was trying to find his murderer. That made me his friend, didn't it?

"I saw him once, a couple of weeks before he died. He called and asked if he could drop by. I said he could."

"Why did he want to see you?"

"He wanted to check out some photos."

"Photos?"

"Yep. I'm the forest ranger that located his old man. I photographed the site. Always do my own pictures, just in case."

I unwound the cord from my wrist. "So he came to see you?"

"Sure did."

"What happened?" I paced along the back of the sofa.

"He looked at the prints, asked me a couple of questions, then raced out of the house like a grizzly was on his tail."

I stood up straight. "Can Darren and I come by and look at the photos?"

"They aren't pretty. The men were smashed up bad by the fall."

"We can handle it."

"Tomorrow's my day off. Come by any time." He gave me an address outside of Tahoe City, and we hung up.

I felt a surge of hope. The pictures might show something that would help Darren. I scrunched the note into my pocket and walked out of the library.

Chapter 9

When I hadn't heard from Darren by ten the next morning, I pulled out a lodge canoe and paddled onto the lake. I'd just moved into an easy motion with the paddles when a noise exploded on shore. A loud crack. Then a zing and a splash to my right. Someone was shooting at me! The paddles banged next to me as I hit the floor. My heart thumped so hard I thought it would break through my rib cage onto the floorboards.

I folded my arms over the back of my head. The damp, sharp wood of the boat dug into my face. I waited to feel an explosion in my back, to feel pain, to die. But all I heard was an occasional honk of a duck or buzz of an insect. The sun beat down on my back. Water lapped against the sides of the canoe.

I waited for what seemed like hours. Trickles of sweat ran down my neck and chest. Finally I raised my head and looked around. The canoe had drifted to the center of the lake. I studied the lodge, then the shore. No one. Had the shooter hidden behind a pine tree? Had the person been aiming at me, or was it an accident? I didn't know, and there was nothing I could do about it.

I picked up the paddles and rowed as hard as I could toward Darren's house, but I couldn't go very fast because my arms were stiff and my hands were numb from holding them over my head all that time.

I was glad to see Darren on the dock. He sat with his elbows propped up on his knees, peering through binoculars aimed at Moon Island. I checked out the weathered boards of the dock. No rifle. I rowed the canoe alongside.

He turned toward me, lowered the binoculars, and got to his feet. "What's wrong?"

Did I look upset? Yeah, probably. After all, I'd just been shot at. "You didn't hear a loud noise a while back, did you?"

"Like what?"

I tied up the boat and climbed onto the dock. "Like a gunshot."

"A shot?" He frowned. "No. But I was working on the Bayliner's engine. You heard a shot?"

"Yes. About a half-hour ago."

"It's probably one of the lodge people taking target practice."

"Yeah, probably." With me as the target? Don't get paranoid, I told myself. It was probably some kid goofing around. There were a couple of real brats staying at the lodge. But how would they have gotten hold of a rifle?

I stood next to him by the boat and slid my palm back and forth along the aluminum rail.

"What happened yesterday at the police station?"

He turned away.

"Come on, Darren. What did the police say?"

He shot me a fierce look. "I got booked."

"What does that mean?"

"It means they arrested me for murder. They're convinced that explosion was set on purpose. They think I killed Brad."

I swallowed hard. "I'm really sorry. Do they have evidence?"

He shrugged. If the police had something on him, he wasn't going to tell me. "What happens now?"

"I've got a hearing a week from Monday. I had to call my parents. They wired the bail, or I'd be in jail right now. My father said he and my mom would try to finish things up and come home soon, but I don't think he meant it. Even my parents don't believe me." He pounded the rail with his fist. "Everyone thinks I'm a murderer."

"I don't." But my words didn't sound convincing, even to me. "Do you have a lawyer?"

"His name is Dan Franks. He's about the only criminal lawyer I know of around here."

"He'll help you."

"Don't count on it. I heard a couple of cops call him Death Row Dan."

I cleared my throat. "What were you looking at through the field glasses?" I asked him.

He slipped the glasses into the pocket of his sweatshirt. "Hoping to spot an eagle."

"Are there some up there?"

"They used to nest on the island."

"And now?"

"They don't go there anymore."

"Why not?"

He scowled at me. "Because Brad shot one. That's why not."

"What?" I took a step back and stared at him. "Did you say Brad shot an eagle?"

"That's what I said." He grabbed the rail of the Bayliner and shoved hard. Water sloshed onto the dock as the boat bounced up and down under the strength of Darren's arm. "I could have killed him for that." The words hung between us, shocking and cold as the water spilling over my feet.

I grabbed the rail, steadying the boat, and stared up at him. "Why would Brad do something so horrible?"

His eyes were puffy and red. "He said he had to have the talons."

"The talons? That's bizarre. Why did he want the talons?"

"How should I know? Something to do with Indian lore. Let's drop it."

"But why—?"

"Drop it, okay?"

"All right." But my head spun with this latest news about Brad. Obviously, he wasn't as mellow as Darren made out. Sometimes the only thing Brad understood was a fist to the jaw, Darren had said. Brad could get Darren riled up. Had he made other people mad, too? "Darren, I talked to Ron Yarrow last night. He has pictures of the accident that killed Brad's and Karen's dads. We've got to go see him. He said Brad took one look at them, asked a couple of questions, and then ran out of the house."

"Seeing pictures of my dad's corpse would make me take off, too." Darren rubbed his eyes.

"Listen to me. There's got to be something in those pictures. Let's go right now."

He frowned. "You really think it's important?"

"Yes."

"All right." Darren moved slowly away from the boat. "I hope it's worth it."

I told him more about my conversation with Ron Yarrow as we walked to his pickup truck. We climbed into the cab, and Darren shoved in a tape. Classical music boomed into the truck as we bumped over the rough road leading out of Sapphire Lake to Lake Tahoe. I was glad for the loud music. It took my mind off the rifle shot that had come so close to me.

I tapped my fingers on my knees. "I thought James was the only person who liked this classical stuff."

He smiled the crooked smile I was beginning to get used to. "It grows on you."

"Convince me."

He was quiet for a while. "Think of the music as the ocean. Sunlight hitting the water, foam flying into the air, waves booming."

"Not bad." I grinned at him and tried to picture

the scene in the music. Me on my surfboard, a hot, sunny day, and the water sparkling like a million diamonds. I could almost see it. "Darren, what's the most beautiful thing you've ever seen?"

He looked ahead at the road, but I could tell he was seeing something else in his mind. "That's easy. An eagle flying over the mountains. The light hits those wings, and it's like something straight out of heaven."

"I've never seen an eagle. It must be awesome."

"I keep thinking that if the eagles came back, everything would be good again. My life would straighten out. I'd have my face back, and the other part of me, too—the part I lost when Brad died. Crazy, huh?"

"No, it's not crazy."

We drove for a while without saying anything, and the music eased into something soft and trilling. Darren turned to me. "Thanks."

"For what?"

"For not thinking I'm a murderer."

I looked quickly away. "No problem."

"Why are you helping me?"

"Because you helped me once. Remember Taffy?"

"Karen's cat?"

"Yes."

"You mean the time I found her for you under the house?"

"You do remember."

He smiled. "You were howling so loud, they

could hear you on top of Devil's Tail. Sure I remember."

I laughed. "Well, anyway, I always appreciated it." But there was more to remember about Darren. Something more from that summer. Except I couldn't bring it back, no matter how hard I tried. Like chasing a ray of sun on the ocean. It kept flitting away from me. "What happened to Taffy, anyway? Did they give her away? Karen said her father decided he didn't want any cats around."

"No. The cat just disappeared one day. Karen moped around for weeks afterward."

"Do you think a wild animal got her?"

"I don't know. Personally, I've always thought Stefan took her to the pound."

"That's awful!" I twisted in the seat. "What a rotten thing to do."

"He could be a nasty guy. A few times, when Karen screwed up a dive or something, he'd chew her out in front of all her friends. It was embarrassing."

"Geez. My dad would never do anything like that."

"You're lucky."

"I know it."

We bumped over a rut in the road. "I hope you don't regret helping me, Megan," he said.

I squeezed my hands over my knees. "Why would I?"

"I don't know." He turned up the volume on the radio, eased into a wide turn, and we shot onto the main highway. The music crashed around us now, making it impossible to talk. Lake Tahoe blurred on our right as we passed trucks hauling lumber and station wagons filled with families and camping gear. Darren drove his truck like he handled the boat, in control but fast enough to make me glad I was wearing a shoulder belt.

In Tahoe City, he veered off the highway. We followed Ron Yarrow's directions down a winding road to a cabin with a yard full of pines. A big man dressed in a flannel shirt and jeans sat on a tree stump, cleaning a fishing reel. I jumped out of the truck and crunched over the ground toward him. Darren was right behind me. The man smiled through a thick, black mustache. If he was shocked at Darren's scars, he didn't show it.

"Mr. Yarrow?" I asked.

"Yep. You here for the pictures?"

"Yes. I'm Megan Delandry and this is Darren Rourke."

Yarrow reached into his shirt pocket. "I was expecting you, so I've got the photos right here. I had an extra set made after Brad called. You can keep these."

"Thanks." Darren took the fat envelope.

"We appreciate it," I added.

"Glad to do it. I was real sorry to hear about Brad. Only met the kid once, but still . . ."

Darren started to walk away.

"Wait," I said. "Mr. Yarrow, you said Brad asked you a couple of questions before he left. Do you remember what he asked you?"

"Yeah, I remember. He wanted to know if the police would be investigating the accident. I said no."

"Anything else?"

He scratched his chin. "Yep. He asked me if I knew any good criminal lawyers. That question really surprised me."

"Criminal lawyers?" Darren's face was as tight as a mask.

"And did you?" I asked.

"I told him that Sam Hargrove was as good as they come."

"Never heard of him," Darren said.

Yarrow leaned forward on the stump. "Sam's semiretired. Only takes a few cases now. But he cuts through the system like a Bowie knife through snow."

"You wouldn't happen to have his phone number, would you? " I asked.

"No, but it's in the book," said the forest ranger. "He practices out of his home in South Lake Tahoe."

"Okay," I said. "Thanks."

"You kids take care now," Yarrow said.

"We will." I waved as we walked back to Darren's pickup.

We drove for about a quarter of a mile in silence. My mind was buzzing with questions about Brad, but my instincts told me to let Darren take the lead. Finally he pulled over and killed the engine. "Let's take a look at those photos."

I nodded. "You first."

He pulled off the rubber band and reached into the envelope. He stared at the photo on top. The sharp intake of breath gave away his reaction. A squirrel chattered in the tree near my open window. "No wonder Brad took off," Darren finally said. "You remember Stefan?" He pointed to the mangled body of a tall, blond man. "That's him. And that's Tom Houston."

"Oh, God." The corpses lay broken on the rocky ground, smashed and bloodied by the fall that had crushed the life out of them. The mens' packs had burst open. Torn clothes and gear hung on rocks and tree branches like crepe paper streamers. "Do you see anything?" I asked Darren. "Anything that could help?"

He shook his head and passed me another photo. "From what Mr. Yarrow told us, it sounds like Brad might have suspected foul play," I said.

"Nah. I bet he just had to know the gory details. I'd do the same if it were my father."

"I never could." The next picture showed a clear view of ripped flesh and clothing. A distance shot showed the high, narrow ledge from which they'd fallen.

I looked over at Darren. "You sure this was an accident? Remember, you thought the boat explosion was an accident, too. Don't you think it's weird that he'd ask about a lawyer?"

He paused. "I can think of one reason why he might have done that. Maybe somebody was threatening to prosecute him for shooting the eagle."

I took my time answering. "Yeah. That could be."

Darren was quiet for a while, staring at the photos. "Stefan and Tom always pushed the envelope. You know, the macho thing. You can bet one of them dared the other to go out on that ledge. They weren't equipped for that kind of climbing. Pure recklessness. That's the reason they died. Besides, who would want to murder them? There's no reason to off two old guys with families."

"You're probably right."

"There are no clues here that I can see." Darren shoved the pictures into the pocket of his jeans and fired up the engine. "Waste of time."

Darren hit the gas pedal, and my head snapped back. He tore down the road to the highway. My shoulder bumped against the door as we flew over a ditch in the asphalt. "Hey, slow down. Are you competing with the Dragster of Death?"

"What's that?"

"My least favorite roller coaster."

"Lay off," he said.

I knew he was upset and tried not to take his bad mood personally, but I wasn't ready to crash and burn, either. "Do me a favor," I yelled. "Slow down to the speed of sound."

But he didn't hear me—or didn't care. We'd gone a couple of miles when a loud noise shrieked behind us. I turned and looked out the window. A police car bore down on us, flashing its lights. "Oh, no," I said.

Darren swore and pounded the steering wheel with his fist. "This is great. Just great." He sped up, and for one panicky second I thought he was going to try to outrun the patrol car. But he wrenched the wheel to the right and brought the truck to a lurching stop on the shoulder. I wiped my palms on my shorts.

He rolled down his window, and we waited in silence as the police officer crunched over the gravel toward us. The cop took off his aviator glasses and gave us a long stare. His name tag read C. Renner. "Did you see the speed limit sign back there?" he asked, in a voice dry as gunpowder.

Darren shook his head.

"You were doing sixty in a forty-five-mile-an-hour zone. I need to see your driver's license and registration."

Darren reached into his jeans and pulled out a battered wallet, then snapped open the glove compartment and rifled through it. He found what he was looking for and silently passed the papers out the window. A breeze blew through the truck, and with it the heavy smell of pine.

The officer studied Darren's license and then looked closely at him. "Hey, you're the kid that Dane and Brady brought in yesterday. Booked and bailed, right? What're you doing in Nevada?"

"Taking a drive," Darren said.

"Uh-huh. Well, Mr. Rourke, crossing the state line from California to Nevada is most likely a violation of your bail terms. Now, why don't you head for the police station in California. I'll follow." His boots crunched against the ground as he marched back to his car.

"Oh, great!" Darren dropped his head to the steering wheel with a thunk as the officer's voice came over the P.A. "Proceed onto the highway. We're right behind you."

My hands squeezed into fists on my knees. "You didn't tell me you were jumping bail, Darren! Why didn't you say something when we drove over the state line? And then you drive like a speed demon. Have you totally lost it?"

He looked at me like I'd slapped him. "I didn't think I'd get caught. But even if I did, it should have been worth it." He started the engine, and we bumped onto the highway, the patrol car on our tail.

"So it's okay to break the law as long as you don't get caught? Is that what you're saying?"

His only answer was a clench of the jaw and a hard grip on the wheel.

Chapter 10

An hour later Darren was in a cell for leaving the state and I was free to go. I punched out the Valaskioff's number with shaking fingers. "Mrs. Thorsten, I need James. I'm at the police station in Tahoe. Please tell him to come right away."

In the parking lot, a landslide of guilt buried me. How could I stand here and breathe the fresh air while Darren was locked up in a cell? If it hadn't been for me pushing him to get the photos, he wouldn't be in jail now. And the pictures hadn't even helped.

When James drove into the lot, I ran over and climbed into the Jeep. "I know you're mad at me for going off with Darren, but I have a good reason."

"The word is angry. And I'm not, Meg." He accelerated onto the highway behind a van hauling two Jet Skis.

The Jeep hit a bump, and we bounced on the seats. "You're not?"

"No. I don't have the right to be angry at you."

I clicked my seat belt on and stared at him. "You're kidding!"

"No."

"I don't get it."

"Then I'll explain it to you." He kept his eyes on the highway. "Anger is one of the ways I try to control you. Julie and I were talking about that this morning. She says that if I cared about you I'd stop protecting you and give you the freedom to find your own divinity."

"What?"

"Your freedom. You know. Like you've been wanting."

"Not that. The other thing you said."

"To find your own divinity?"

"Yeah. Isn't divinity reserved for God?"

"Julie believes we're all part of the same divine matter."

I stuck my finger in my mouth and made a gagging sound.

"That's obnoxious, Meg."

"So are her dumb ideas." I pressed my feet into the floor mat. Sun streamed through the windshield, warming my bare legs. "I can't understand why you're taking her junk seriously, James." Except that Julie's a cute girl, I thought. But so? James knew lots of cute girls, and he wouldn't date anyone who couldn't keep up with him in the brains department.

"Because her ideas are good," he said. "I need to get in touch with my inner power, and so do you."

"Leave me out of this. I don't want anything to do with weird Julie."

"Aren't you being intolerant?"

"The word is intelligent. Remember, James? You used to know what that meant."

He let out an exasperated sigh. "Look, I realize I've been playing the parent with you, Meg. Admit it. I've been driving you crazy."

"Well . . ." I shrugged.

"Things are going to change. From now on, I'll stay off your back. I'm going to focus in on myself."

"Seems to me you're focused in on Julie."

"I am. Her insights are uncanny. And she's strong. She showed me something today that I wouldn't have thought possible, except I saw it for myself."

I rolled my eyes. "And now you're going to tell me."

"You might find it interesting." James was keeping the Jeep right at the speed limit. He hadn't gone completely bonkers. "Julie's family has this barbecue pit behind their house, and you won't believe this . . ."

"Try me."

"She walked on the hot coals, barefoot." He shook his head. "I actually stood there and watched her do it. Her feet weren't even singed."

I squeezed my hands into fists. "You're kidding. Why would she do something like that?"

"To prove that our minds are more powerful than the material world. When we know that, we can do anything."

"James, Julie's a nut case. You thought so yourself the first time we met her."

"I've changed my mind—something you're obviously too stubborn to do."

Why, I asked myself, had my brother changed so much since we'd arrived at Sapphire Lake? "I thought you were the stodgy one, and I liked you better that way."

He swung the Jeep around a slow-moving truck. "I've always done everything that was expected of me. Straight A's. All-city in cross-country. Choir. I'm sick of being Saint James."

I thought for a minute. "Where's Julie getting this power of hers, anyway?"

"I told you. From inside herself."

"I doubt it. Haven't you heard Mom and Dad talk about the ancient sorcerers? Those guys saw the future, walked through fire, you name it. None of the stuff Julie does is new. It's old magic. It goes back to biblical times."

"Thanks for the ancient history lesson, professor."

"Any time." I drummed my fingers on my thigh. "So Julie plays around with fire and doesn't get burned? I wonder how her tricks fit into Brad's murder."

He stared at me for a moment. "Are you saying Julie had something to do with Brad's death?"

"That's what it sounds like to me."

"Think again, Meg. Julie is the gentlest, most nonviolent person I've ever met."

"Oh, yeah? If I were you, I'd drop her like a hot coal."

A muscle twitched in his jaw, and his mouth

pressed into a thin line. I could still get to him. But I was serious this time. I thought I should tell him about the gunshot, but he'd probably only warn me to stay away from Darren. Or maybe this new James wouldn't say anything at all.

When James pulled in behind the lodge and parked the Jeep, I followed him to the bike rack near the front porch. He unlocked his bike and rolled it out of the rack while I gave him the short version of what had happened to Darren and me.

"You know that cop could have arrested Darren as a fugitive," James said. "Another felony. He's lucky the guy didn't roll over him like a tank. And you, too. He could have ordered you out at gunpoint, searched you, cuffed you." James shook his head.

So maybe Officer C. Renner hadn't pegged Darren as a murderer. The thought gave me hope. "Can you help Darren, James? His hearing's next Monday, and he needs a good lawyer."

James turned the bike toward the road and threw one leg over the seat. "I'm a college student, not a lawyer."

He started up the road, and I jogged after him. "But you know how the system works. Can't you do something?"

"No. The police obviously have enough evidence to charge him with murder." He guided the bike around a branch lying in the road. "There's nothing either of us can do."

"I'll think of something." My stomach felt as if I'd caught a wave in storm surf. "Why won't you help him, James? Darren was your friend once."

"Brad was my friend, too, and I was looking forward to seeing him this summer. He wouldn't listen to Julie, and now he's dead."

"Maybe she can still put you in touch with him. The three of you could have a little seance together." I bit my lip in disgust at what I'd just said.

James took off up the road. "You're on your own this time," he yelled over his shoulder.

I stood there, hands on hips. How could he just ride away like that? If only he'd screech to a halt, leap off his bike, and lecture me the way the old James would have. Didn't he care anymore?

I turned back and went into the lodge, heading for the rec room. Grabbing a musty-smelling telephone book off the bookshelf, I located Sam Hargrove's number on Pinetree Lane in South Lake Tahoe. I dialed, and to my surprise, the lawyer himself answered. "Hargrove here, " he said in a voice like a buzz saw.

"Um, Mr. Hargrove?" I twisted the cord around my forearm and did my usual pacing.

"Yes, ma'am?"

"My name's Megan Delandry. I need to ask you a question."

"Shoot, Ms. Delandry."

I was expecting to be grilled with questions and had to think for a second before I spoke. "Did a boy named Brad Houston ever call you? It would have been in the spring some time. Brad was murdered soon after that. I'm a friend of the boy they suspect murdered Brad, Darren Rourke. But I don't think Darren did it, Mr. Hargrove. Could you help him?"

"Whoa, now, one question at a time. Let's start with the first one. Yes, Brad Houston called me. I read about his death in the papers."

"What did he want?"

"Well, Ms. Delandry, you probably know that I can't repeat our conversation. It's privileged information."

"He made an appointment, didn't he?"

There was a long pause, and I could hear him scribbling on a notepad. Probably writing down everything I said. According to James, lawyers always did that. "He might have," he said.

"But he died before he could get in to see you."

He cleared his throat.

"Do the police know he called you?"

"They haven't asked. You're not an undercover cop, are you?" There was a chuckle in his voice, and suddenly I felt about ten years old.

I made my voice lower. "No. Ron Yarrow says you're a great lawyer. Can you help my friend, Darren Rourke?"

There was a long sigh. "I'm afraid not. I've got a lot of cases right now."

"Please, Mr. Hargrove!" Desperation made my voice rise to the ten-year-old level again. "Darren's in jail in Tahoe. Couldn't you just go see him—or call him, anyway? Darren's got no one. He's accused of murder, and he needs help."

"Does he have a lawyer now?"

"Yes. Someone named Dan Franks."

There was a long pause. "I'll think about it, Ms. Delandry. That's all I can promise."

"Okay, Mr. Hargrove. Thanks!" I hung up. Across the room, the cold, dead eyes of the mountain lion stared at me. I turned abruptly and ran out of the lodge, going across the porch and down the steps.

About fifty yards beyond the lodge stood Julie's redbrick house, overlooking the lake. I headed for it. When I got there, I walked around to the front and knocked.

The door opened, and a heavy woman with red hair greeted me. Julie's mother. I introduced myself and asked to see Julie. I was led between flowered couches, past a blaring television set. I checked out everything I could. No rifles in sight. "Julie," she called at the back door. "James's sister is here to see you."

James's sister. My brother was known here in this house. It gave me a spooky feeling, like these people should be my friends. But they weren't. I couldn't imagine ever being friends with Julie. I thought of Kelly, my best friend at home, and all the goofy things we laughed about together— beauty contests, her sister's pet tarantula, guys with tattoos. How could I ever laugh with Julie?

I thanked her mom and walked down the wooden steps, crossing a stretch of brown grass to where Julie lay stretched out on a lounge in the shade. Glass wind chimes hung high in the pine tree, tinkling in the breeze. Julie wore a black bikini that made her skin look the color of skim milk, and she was painting her fingernails with lavender polish. Nearby, the barbecue pit smouldered. I checked the soles of her feet. A little calloused, but otherwise unmarked. "Hi," I said.

She waved a hand in the air, and the smell of nail polish mixed with the smells of pine trees and smoke. The jewel at her neck glowed like a lavender eye. She nodded at the lounge next to her. "Have a seat, Megan."

I plopped down on the white plastic strips, feeling them press into my bare thighs below my shorts. "What're you doing?" Brilliant question.

"My nails."

"Right."

She smiled and looked up at me. "What are *you* doing?"

"I was walking by, and I thought I'd stop in and see you."

"To ask me about my predictions?"

"No."

"What then?" She lifted an eyebrow.

"Where were you when Brad died?" I blurted out.

She smiled as if she'd already known that was why I came. "Does it matter?"

"It might."

She pumped the brush into the bottle and slid the wet bristles over her last two fingernails. Finally she looked up at me with her maple-syrup smile. Why did everything about her remind me of food? I wondered.

"If you're trying to prove that Darren didn't kill Brad, you're going to have a hard time. Only Darren knew that Brad would be alone in the boat that morning. The two of them always rode together. They skied every morning. Same time, same place, except for that morning. And as for the murderer being there or not when it happened, it doesn't matter."

"Why?"

"The engine could have been set to explode beforehand."

"Mmmm . . . I guess you're right."

She set the bottle of polish on the table next to her and waved her wet nails in the air. "Being right is one of my many talents."

"What are the others?" As if I really wanted to know.

"Helping people." She smiled. "You need my help, don't you, Megan?"

I rolled my eyes. "If I needed help, I wouldn't come to you."

"Why not? I've helped a lot of people resolve their inner conflicts." The lounge squeaked as she leaned forward. Her hair fluffed over her shoulders, touching the tops of her knees. "I wish I could help Darren, but he has a stubborn spirit. He isn't open to what I have to teach him."

"What about Brad? Did you try to help him, too?"

"Yes, I tried."

"By predicting he'd die?"

"The crystals told me he was in danger. He wouldn't listen until the end, and then it was too late."

I leveled a stare at her. "Darren seems to think you had something to do with Brad's death."

"What an idea." She checked her nails. "I restore life, not take it away. I was only passing along the message I was given."

"Who gave it to you?"

"The crystals."

"Who killed Brad?"

"The crystals haven't told me that."

"Where were you when it happened?"

"On the island."

"Did anyone see you?"

"No." Her voice was soft. "Only my crystals."

"And they can't talk. At least, not out loud."

"They've told me one thing, Megan." Her eyes caught mine. "You are in terrible danger. That person is getting closer and closer. Someone wants to hurt you."

"Who is it?" My voice sounded higher than usual.

"I don't know, but you teeter on the edge of a precipice. One wrong step, and down you go."

"Why don't you loan me your broomstick, and I'll fly across?"

Julie's laughter tinkled like the wind chimes above us. "You're afraid, aren't you? But insulting me won't take away your fear. It would be wise for you to leave Sapphire Lake—that is, if you

94

wish to continue in your present life."

"And then you glom on to James?"

"Does it bother you that I make your brother happy? After all, you wanted your freedom. I said you would have it, and now you do."

I flipped my hair over my shoulders. "You don't make him happy. My brother isn't himself. He's, well, he's . . ."

"More centered, less ambitious and tense."

"More *self*-centered, you mean." I stared hard at her. "I think he's turning into a big, fat bore, if you want to know the truth."

She touched the jewel at her throat. "James needs to throw off his bonds and be free."

"Am I one of those bonds?"

"I believe you are."

I folded my arms. "James will figure out the truth soon enough."

"What truth?"

"The truth about Brad's death." I was bluffing, but I still had a feeling about her.

"Let me tell you something, Megan." She stood up, and her pale eyes glittered in the shadows of the trees. "The truth is that James belongs to me now. Our union was made many lives ago."

I stood, too, and towered over her. "That's a bunch of baloney."

She smiled. "Are you climbing to Devil's Tail with us next Tuesday? It's an overnight trip, and everyone's going. Except Darren, of course."

Hadn't she just warned me about staying away

from high places? And now she was prompting me to go? I thought of the photos, the men's smashed and bloody bodies, and fear wound its way up my spine. "I didn't know about the trip."

"Hello, ladies." I turned quickly. My brother bounded down the back steps toward us. He didn't look a bit unhappy. In fact, his smile was so broad, it looked silly. His brown hair, usually combed straight back, flopped over his forehead. I hadn't really noticed before, but his teeth were perfect. White and even. All those years of braces had really paid off. "Ready for that sail, Julie? There's a good wind kicking up."

"Yes. Let's take the Hobie Cat." She turned to me. "Megan, would you like to come along?"

"No," I said. "You guys have fun. See you later." My arm brushed against James's as I passed him.

Once out in front of Julie's house, I ran past the lodge, down the road, and past the archery range. I sped by Brad's house and Darren's, but finally I had to slow to a fast walk to catch my breath. Was Julie right about me being in danger? Had someone meant to hit me with that bullet earlier today? I didn't want to believe her, but she did seem to know things. Could what I told James be true? Was she tapping in to the same power that the ancient sorcerers had used to see into the future? If so, it wasn't just me who was in danger. It was all of us.

Chapter 11

*B*ack at the lodge, I checked out the rifle case. All of the guns were in place behind the smudged glass. Let it go for a while, I told myself.

On the counter in the front lobby, there were letters for James and me from Mom and Dad. I ripped mine open and read that everything was going well with the dig, that they'd uncovered some valuable artifacts. If all went as planned, they'd be home early in September. I took the letter with me to the beach that afternoon and read it over a few more times. It made me feel like Mom and Dad weren't so far away.

I spent the rest of the afternoon on the beach and the next morning headed back to the empty cove, where I stayed until noon, waiting for the facts to click together in my brain and make some kind of sense. It was sunny and hot, and my mind drifted back and forth like the currents on the lake. Finally hunger overcame my determination to solve the puzzle, and I headed up to the lodge for lunch.

At the big table in the kitchen, I joined a couple of little kids and their mom for peanut butter and jelly sandwiches and lemonade. It turned out they lived in Santa Monica, too, so we had a lot to talk about. After we ate, I ran upstairs, showered, and pulled on a tank top and cutoffs. Then I wandered out to the dock, where I found Karen putting away fishing equipment. She was dressed in one of her red Valaskioff T-shirts and shorts.

I watched her polish the windshield on the Chris Craft and after some small talk asked her if she'd heard a rifle shot yesterday morning.

"No." She whipped her rag against the glass. "But I was up at Desolation with the Llewellyns, fishing for trout." She looked at me with a frown. "If someone's shooting around here, I want to hear about it. And if they're lodge guests, they'll be gone."

"Could it be someone target shooting?"

She rubbed at a blur on the edge of the glass. "No way. Any shooting would be too dangerous this time of year, with tourists wandering in and out of here. It's off-limits for lodge guests. If you see or hear anything more, be sure to tell me."

"I'll let you know if I hear anything else."

"I don't mean to sound like a hardnose, but we need to look out for everybody who stays with us."

"I know that." I watched her rub for a while, feeling like I ought to help, but just as I was about to say something, she folded the rag and slipped it under the windshield.

"How about that archery lesson?" I asked.

"Sure thing." She grinned. "I guess I'm as good a teacher as Roberto."

"Is he baby-sitting again?"

"Yeah. Kids, what a pain."

"I don't know. I kind of like the little monsters." I thought of the volleyball team I coached at home. The kids drove me crazy, but I missed them, too. Suddenly I was homesick for our house and the sight of the ocean. I missed Mom and Dad like crazy. The feelings stayed with me as we walked to the storage shed and picked out bows and arrows.

At the target range, Karen showed me how to hold the weapon. My first few shots zinged past the bale of hay, but finally I hit it. "This is harder than I thought," I told her. "How did you get so good?"

She barked out a laugh. "I had to."

"What do you mean?"

"Father. He decided I had to be a Valkyrie."

"What's that?"

"A Norse warrior goddess."

"Seriously?"

"You've heard of Brynhild? Well, that's the idea. We go back to Scandinavian royalty, and Father insisted that I learn all the royal skills. He taught me how to hunt with a bow, ski, mountain-climb. I had to practice until I got all of it right."

I remembered what Darren had said about her father humiliating her in front of her friends. Thinking back to that other summer, I vaguely remembered him ordering her to dive off the dock and swim to a raft. She'd cried, but he hadn't backed off. "What if you didn't? Get it right?"

She smiled. "He'd give me a wallop, leave me alone on the mountain—whatever it took."

"That's awful!"

"Yeah, but look at me now." She held up her bow. "I can do it all. And people know it."

Just for a second, she did resemble a Norse goddess, with her strong body and blond hair shining in the sun. Her bow looked lethal, and her red T-shirt was printed with the usual white shield. Any minute now, she'd leap on her steed and ride off to war.

She lowered the bow. "Once, a writer came to the lodge and interviewed me for a story on the Sierras. Some day the Valaskioff will be famous. We've already had a couple of bigwigs here. Actors and stuff. They think it's cool to have a girl guide. Thanks to my dear father, I can handle myself anywhere, anytime."

I thought of Dad and how gentle he'd always been with me. He never forced me into anything and even tried to keep his cool when my grades weren't so hot. "What did Brad think about your dad treating you that way?"

"His dad was a hardnose, too. Best hunter in the Sierras. It made us tough. In Brad's case, though, not tough enough." She looked away.

"You must miss him a lot."

"Yeah, we had lots of plans. We wanted to open a wilderness school, take all the rich tourists out and teach them survival skills." She wiped her eyes. "We even asked our dads to lend us the money to start the school. But they said no.

They said we were too young, can you believe it?"

"Well, you are pretty young to start your own business."

"Brad was ticked. He said he wished he could think of some way to get his hands on his dad's money right away."

"No kidding?"

Karen looked away quickly, as if aware that she'd said too much.

Excitement ran up my spine at her disclosure, and I felt I had to act right away. "I guess Brad must have taken after his father, right?"

She gave me a sharp look. "What do you mean?"

"He liked to kill animals."

"Where did you hear that?"

"Darren told me he killed an eagle."

"Hunters hunt, Megan. That's how it is up here."

"Not eagles they don't. That's illegal, and you know it."

"Darren's trying to make Brad look bad to you." She marched to the target and started ripping out arrows.

"Then it's not true?" I joined her at the bale of hay. "He didn't kill an eagle?"

"Maybe, but Brad had his reasons."

"What were they?"

"It's not really your business."

I'd upset her, but I wasn't retreating yet. "How did Roberto feel about Brad killing the eagle? Was he mad?"

"You'll have to ask him."

"I will."

"I bet Darren didn't tell you about the ski contest, did he?"

"What ski contest?"

"The one Brad won right before he died. Darren punched him for it. Knocked him out cold. Everybody thought Brad was dead for a minute, until he recovered. Even then, he didn't see through Darren. He told me he was going to help Darren practice his dock start the next morning. I couldn't talk him out of it. And now he's dead! I'm going to tell the D.A. every rotten thing Darren ever did to Brad. Maybe the jury will have more sense than you, Megan. Maybe they'll give Darren what he deserves. Maybe he'll even get the death penalty."

"Don't say that, Karen."

"Look, I know you have a crush on the guy. But it's time to wise up. Ask him about the ski contest."

"I will, if I ever see him again. And I don't have a crush on him."

She jerked an arrow free. "For your own good, I hope you don't. By the way, did James tell you we're climbing Devil's Tail next week? Tuesday's the day."

I grabbed a wooden shaft and pulled it from the straw. "Julie mentioned it."

"You want to come? It'll get your mind off Darren and all this stuff. Julie's going to have a session up there. It should be dynamite."

I frowned. "I don't know."

Karen's blue eyes pierced mine. "Julie really psyched you out with her warning, didn't she?"

"Like she psyched Brad out?"

"If he was scared of anyone, it was Darren, not Julie."

"That's not what I heard." Maybe it was getting caught for murder that scared Brad. Could he have been involved in his father's death? Would he have confided in Karen if he was? And even if he did, would she tell me? If I kept asking questions, she might stop talking to me altogether.

She stuffed the arrows into her quiver. "Let me know if you decide to go on the hike. I need to get our supplies together. It'll be an overnighter."

"Okay."

As much as I hated the thought of climbing that mountain, I realized that I might have to do it. I would need every opportunity, it seemed, to find out all I could about Brad's friends. One of them, I was sure, had murdered Brad. I didn't want to believe it was Darren.

Chapter 12

I called the jail several times over the next few days, but Darren wouldn't talk to me. On Monday morning after breakfast, I hurried to the library and dialed the number from there.

The woman who answered said she'd call Darren. I stared out the library window as I waited. The light caught a branch of a pine tree, turning the needles to gold. The jays screeched back and forth like kids playing games in the forest.

Darren's low, hoarse voice came through the receiver. "Megan? Why do you keep calling me?"

The pine branch brushed the window with its gold bristles. "Don't you know by now?"

"Morbid curiosity?" I could almost see his shoulders hunching and the scowl on his face.

"No." I pressed the receiver against my ear. "Friendship."

"I don't need friends. That's how I got into this mess in the first place. My friends will strap me down for the lethal injection and party in the viewing room."

"You're already having a pity party. Has anyone called you besides me?"

"No."

"Listen, I'll come to visit you. We'll figure out some way to get you out of there."

"Thanks for the offer, but I'll take care of it myself." His voice was cold.

"What do you mean? Do you have a plan?"

"No. Forget it. Look, I've got to go. Don't bother calling me again. I won't come to the phone."

"Darren, wait!"

"What?"

"Did you know that Brad called the lawyer—Mr. Hargrove?"

"No."

"What do you think it means?"

"I think he was worried about the eagle business, like I told you."

"Uh-huh. One more thing." I paused for breath. "Did you hit Brad and knock him out after he beat you in the ski contest?"

There was a silence before he answered. "Yeah, I hit Brad."

"Why?"

"It's not important."

"Yes, it is. Why did you do it?"

"I told you. Sometimes all Brad understood was a fist to the jaw." His voice broke. "I loved Brad, but the guy could get to me. Everybody knew that. It doesn't mean I killed him."

"What did he do, Darren? What got to you?"

"Good-bye, Megan. Don't call again." He was gone.

I slammed down the receiver. How could I help him when he wouldn't even help himself? Why did I want to help him, anyway? Was Karen right? Did I still have a crush on him? Or had the crush turned to something else? Maybe I just had to know the truth to satisfy my curiosity. The nose in action. I felt a pang, remembering James's old name for me, and walked outside. As if my thoughts had produced him, there was my brother, sitting by himself on the porch.

I plopped down on the swing next to him. "Hi, big brother."

"Morning."

I waited for him to say more, but he just stared out at the lake. "How's weird Julie?" I asked.

He frowned. "Meg, stop."

I folded my arms. "She's involved in Brad's death somehow, James."

He turned to me and pushed up his glasses. "Got any evidence?"

"No, just a gut feeling."

"Gut feelings don't stand up in court." He took a deep breath. "This is really funny, you know? You warning me about Julie. It should be the other way around."

"You mean Darren?"

"Who else?"

"I know it looks like he's guilty. I don't think he is, though. He's scared, and, well, angry, because nobody will believe him."

"Except you."

"Yes," I said. "Except me."

He gripped the armrest on the swing. "I'm glad you're here, Meg. I've been wanting to tell you something for the past week." His eyes were serious behind the blurred glass of his horn-rims. "I've made a decision."

A tingle of fear pricked my spine. "What?"

"I'm dropping out of the university and staying at Sapphire Lake this winter. I need a break, to get in tune with nature and myself, find out who I really am and what I really want. And spend more time with Julie."

"*What*?" Shock made me dumb. "You can't! Mom and Dad'll never let you do this, James."

"They don't have a choice."

"And besides, you *know* who you are. At least you did until we came up here."

"I've changed, and I have a lot more changing to do. Admit it, Meg. You couldn't stand me before I met Julie."

"That's not true."

"Yes, it is." He gave me a wry smile and stood up, moving toward the steps. "I'm staying here. I've made up my mind."

"I did like you before," I called after him as he walked down the steps and up the road toward Julie's house. "I just didn't realize it." It was all I could do not to chase after him and try to pound some sense into him with my fists. But Julie was right about one thing. You couldn't force people to do things just because you wanted them to.

I ran down to the docks and grabbed a canoe, paddling out onto the lake. The gentle rush of water along the boat calmed me. I decided to cross the lake to Roberto's house. Twenty minutes later, I maneuvered my canoe between a windsurfer and a catamaran, tied it up, and jumped onto the dock, walking toward Roberto's log mansion.

A giant, barking dog bounded around the side of the house, straight at me. I froze.

"Lobo!" Roberto ran across the yard after the monster. It thundered over the dock. I stepped backward, but there was no way I could reach the canoe before the beast was on me. I screamed.

"He's friendly," Roberto yelled.

A cold, wet nose hit my arm.

"He'll lick you to death is all."

My breath heaved out as the dog jumped up and shoved two paws into my chest. I stumbled backward. A long red tongue shot out and sloshed across my nose. "Down boy," I wheezed. The dog sat at my feet and wiggled its hind quarters. "Nice doggie," I croaked. My heart hammered in my chest. The dog's tail swept across the boards of the dock, raising dust like a push broom.

"Sorry." Roberto jogged up to me. "He's an overgrown pup."

"What kind is he?" My voice sounded squeaky.

"German shepherd." Roberto scratched the dog's ears. "But he looks like a wolf, don't you, Lobo, baby?"

"Definitely." I took a deep breath and let my fingers brush the dog's head while my heart slowed down. "Have you got a minute?"

"For what? More questions about Brad?"

"Would that bother you?"

He shrugged.

I smiled. "If I get too nosy, you can always sic your dog on me."

He laughed. "To be straight, I've got the day. Mom's got Jesse and Gus. Doctor appointments and then a movie. Why don't we crash for a while?" He walked to the end of the dock in his long, graceful stride with Lobo at his heels and unfolded two beach chairs. We sank into them. The big shepherd stretched out near a large wooden storage chest. Something inside caught a gleam of sunlight through a crack in the wood. Lobo's tail thumped on the dock.

Out on the lake, two Jet Skis whined a duet into the air. The sun burned into our skin. Roberto let his head fall back as he gazed at the sky. His long hair was pulled into a ponytail, and the dark strands dangled over the back of the chair. A jet streaked overhead, leaving a trail of silent white. We sat there for a long time, peace wrapping around us like a warm blanket.

Finally I broke the silence. "The mountains are beautiful this morning. Like gray castles in the sky."

"That's a great picture," Roberto said. "But those mountains are killers. Remember the Donner party?"

"Didn't they get caught in a pass during winter and run out of food?"

"Yeah. Donner Lake's not far, about twenty-five miles. They ended up cannibals. Killed the two Indian guides who helped them out. Pigged out on their hides and each others'."

"Ugh. Gross."

"I heard you're climbing with us Tuesday," Roberto said.

"I haven't decided yet. I want to ask you something—"

"Devil's Tail is a tough climb," he interrupted.

I stared up at the arrowhead-shaped peak, and for a minute I lost my train of thought. "That's what I hear." I pulled off my T-shirt and stripped to my bathing suit, baring my shoulders and back to the sun. "Roberto, what do eagle talons mean to you?"

He looked sharply at me. "Why?"

"I heard that Brad shot an eagle for its talons. I thought you might know why."

"That creep." His voice was low and furious.

I stared hard at him. "What does it mean?"

He looked up at Devil's Tail Peak. "My ancestors believed the talons had the power to ward off evil."

"And Brad knew that?"

"Yeah, and he knew the eagle was sacred to my family. But that didn't stop him from killing it."

"Did he do it because he was scared?" I'd keep asking as long as he'd answer. He didn't seem to mind my questions as much this morning.

He pressed his lips together in a tight line. "It doesn't matter. He was doomed after that. Karen is better off without him." The wind lifted a loose strand of hair and blew it across his cheekbone. He did look like an Indian warrior with his dark eyes and skin.

"Did you threaten to report Brad?"

"No threats. I did report him."

So maybe Darren was right, I thought. That was why Brad had contacted Mr. Hargrove.

Roberto leaned forward, staring at me. "You planning to visit Darren in jail?"

"I want to, but he told me not to come. James won't take me into town, anyway."

"You like him, don't you?"

I shrugged. "He needs a friend."

"Be careful. I like him, too, but . . ."

"But what?"

He shrugged. "The guy's wild. My folks won't let him in our house anymore."

I stared at him. "Why not?"

"My dad hates him."

"Why?" I leaned forward. "What did he do?"

"A couple of years ago, Dad got a new Camaro. Red."

"Wow!"

"Yeah. It *was* a wow before Darren got ahold of it. A bunch of the guys were over one day after school. Older guys. I was real impressed, you know, that they'd want to spend time with me. Darren started in about the car. I shouldn't have done it, but I let him take it for a drive. He swore somebody cut him off . . ."

"What happened?" I pushed back my hair.

"He crashed it. Totaled it. The insurance didn't

cover him, so my Dad was out a ton of money. He came down like a wall of granite on me, and he hasn't let Darren off the hook yet, even though he paid my dad back with money he earned working for the movie company."

"Was he drunk?"

"Nope. Darren drinks soda. He's trouble, that's all."

"I don't think his parents care much about him. They seem really caught up in doing their own thing."

"Yeah. You're right about that."

"He's the most intense guy I've ever met. That's why I like him."

"He can lose it real fast."

"Like the time he hit Brad?"

"He went nuts. The next day Brad was history."

"Have you seen him hurt anyone else?"

He thought for a while. "No."

"Do you think Brad was afraid of Darren?"

"Brad ran everything and everybody until Julie psyched him out with her prediction."

I pulled a bottle of suntan oil from the pocket of my shorts and rubbed it on my legs. "So Brad acted different than usual before he died?"

"You could say that. He turned from mellow to crazy overnight. The guy had never had any mercy for animals, but to kill an eagle . . ." His eyes were hard and dark as night.

I set the suntan oil on the dock. "It had to be Julie's prediction that scared Brad so much. If someone told me I'd die within the month, it would worry me, too." Stay away from high places. That's what she'd told me.

"Maybe it was both. Darren and Julie."

"I don't think so, but I'm going to find out."

"Good luck, Megan."

"Thanks." But I wondered if he really meant it.

A harsh noise blasted my ears, and it took a second before I realized it was Lobo barking. The big dog leaped into the air, snapping, snarling, and baring its teeth.

"What—?" I half-rose from my chair as Roberto let out a yell.

There was a flutter of wings, the flash of black feathers, and a big black bird soared away.

"Aaaaeeehhhh!" Roberto dropped to his knees on the dock.

I moved next to him. "Roberto, what's wrong? It was only a hawk. It's gone now."

He hugged Lobo around the neck, buried his face in the big dog's fur, and rocked back and forth. His long, low cries gave me the creeps.

"What's the matter, Roberto? Tell me." I held his shaking shoulders.

He turned to look at me, and his dark eyes glittered. "Death. It's coming. Someone's going down."

"No." I drew back. "You can't believe that."

"I don't want to. But it dove straight at us. And there are no more eagles to fight the evil. My dream told me this would happen."

"Birds don't control good and evil, Roberto, you know that. People do." I looked at his tearstreaked face, and my stomach knotted. "No one's going to die," I said.

He turned away. I knew he was embarrassed for crying in front of me, and I let him be while he composed himself.

Minutes passed as we sat there, absorbed in our own thoughts. In the distance, Devil's Tail cut into the sky. How would it feel, climbing up that sheer peak? I thought again of the photographs and the mangled bodies of the men. Maybe I should forget the whole thing.

When I turned back to Roberto, he'd wiped the tears from his face and was sprawled in his chair, staring at me. He looked as cool as always. "You climbing with us?" he asked.

I tensed at the switch in his emotions. Was he hiding something? Or maybe putting on a show to keep me away from the mountain?

I pulled back a little under his knowing eyes. "Why are you hiking, Roberto? Karen said climbing bores you."

"Because she asked me to. She hasn't been to Devil's Tail since her father died. She wants me there."

"Karen and Stefan had kind of a strange relationship, didn't they?"

"He could be tough."

"How can she go up to Devil's Tail, knowing he died there?"

"As long as they run the lodge, she'll have to take climbers up."

"Yeah. James really pushed for this hike, but I

don't think he's even thought about her dad. All he thinks about is Julie."

"Julie has that effect on some guys," Roberto said.

"But not you or Brad or Darren?"

"No."

"Why not?"

"I don't know. Just not our type, I guess." I saw a flush creep up his cheeks, and I knew he was thinking of Karen.

Roberto and I swam and lay in the sun until his mom and brothers came home late that afternoon. When I'd said good-bye and was sure they were all inside the house, I moved quickly to the storage bin on the edge of the dock and raised the lid.

I pulled away the canvas covering and reached inside, where I'd seen the glimmer of light. My hand closed around something smooth and cold, and I knew what it was even before I pulled it out into the light. The polished wood and steel rifle was the same as Darren's, but below the Winchester insignia the initials were different— BJH. Bradley J. Houston.

Chapter *13*

I sat up in bed, gasping for breath, my heart racing. The dream again. This time the face had come up to meet me. Its grinning jaws were about to devour me. I woke up, and there were tears on my cheeks. I felt like a terrified kid. But I was too old to yell for Mom and Dad, like I had the summer I was seven. I wiped my face, slipped out of bed, and walked to the window.

The lake was bright under the stars. I could barely make out the Bayliner docked at Darren's place. How long would he be in jail? Maybe forever.

Something moved on the island. A flash of white. Was Julie up there with her crystals? And was James with her? My brother was right. I was too nosy for my own good. Another movement caught my eye, like something was being lifted off the ground. What was going on up there?

I pulled on my jeans under my nightshirt and yanked my sweatshirt from the rocker where I'd thrown it earlier. The clock read 1:36 A.M. I remembered something Dad said once. "All people, in all cultures, instinctively fear the hours between midnight and three in the morning. It's the time for evil, human and supernatural." I'd told Roberto that dreams could be messages. What was my dream trying to tell me?

I glanced at the portrait over the desk. The knight's face, dimly lit by moonlight, looked like it was made out of plastic. *Like a mask.* I sat on the bed, shocked at the sudden idea. I breathed slowly in and out, trying to stay calm. Was that what the face in my dream was? Dad collected books on ancient religions, and one of them had dozens of pictures of masks. Symbols of demonic spirits. There was some kind of danger out there, waiting for me.

My fingers shook as I tied my hair back, but I forced myself to go to the door. The knob turned easily. I tiptoed down the hall, stopping at James's room, and pressed my ear to his door. Soft snores came from inside. Good. I continued to the stairs. The huge mansion was quiet.

Why are you doing this? I asked myself. I wanted to turn around and go back to the safety of my bed, but if I waited until tomorrow, James would be glued to Julie, and I wanted to catch her alone, in the act.

But what act? I didn't know. I just had a feeling that she was a part of everything that had happened at the lake. I crept down the stairs and across the wide entry hall to the front door. The bolt slid back smoothly, and I pushed the door open. The porch lay hidden in shadows.

I crept down the path to the beach. The dock creaked under my feet. I looked back at the Valaskioff. The windows were dark. Everyone slept.

My canoe slid easily into the water. The lightweight boat lurched violently as I stepped in and lowered myself onto the damp seat. Finally, it stabilized. The paddles made soft splashes under my hands.

Moonlight carved outlines of mansions in the dark pines. Insect noises squeaked into the night as I glided toward the island. A muffled shriek came from the forest, and I imagined a small furry victim being attacked by something big and hungry. Deep barks echoed over the water. Lobo must have heard the hapless animal, too. The canoe bumped onto the beach, and I hopped out and ran across the sand to the mountain path.

I took the trail we'd taken our first night at Sapphire Lake. The altitude didn't bother me anymore, but the long drop at my back still made my knees shake. Any minute I expected to feel hands on my shoulders, pushing me. Don't think about it, I told myself. Just keep climbing.

At the top, I looked around. I saw nothing but the dark pines. I heard nothing but the squeaks of insects.

The meadow grass was interspersed with pebbles, twigs, and pinecones. Across the lake, Devil's Tail stabbed through clouds. The night air was cold and still. What had I expected to find up here? A super-seance with Julie spilling her guts about Brad's murderer? I checked quickly behind me to make sure no one was there.

The air smelled different—like pines, but something else, too. Winter. Fires in the fireplace. I crisscrossed the area until I found a mound of dirt. I pressed my palm lightly against it. Warm. Someone had recently built a fire at the edge of the pines.

A sudden whirring noise came from behind me. I whipped around. The forest was black. Was it an animal stalking something in the woods—or a person?

And then it came. A screech that pierced the air and sent waves of terror through me. *I have to get out of here! Now!* I took short, jerky steps back across the clearing. Moonlight lit the ground. Several large scratches were visible in the dirt, fresh and deep. My breath caught in my throat, and I nearly choked. *Those claw marks weren't there before!*

The screech came again. Louder. Closer. I got to the path, knocking pebbles and roots down the hill ahead of me and scratching my hands as I sat down and skidded on my rear as fast as I could toward the beach.

My canoe! Where was it? I ran across the sand. It had to be here! I looked out at the lake. No sign of it.

Something grabbed my shoulder. I screamed and spun around.

Darren stood there, his face a horror mask in the moonlight. *Mask. Oh, God, no.*

I stared at him, frozen into silence.

"Hello, Megan." The low, husky voice was his, not an evil spirit's.

"What are you doing here?" I whispered.

"Your canoe was drifting away." He pointed, and I saw a silver hull peeking out from the bushes. "I grabbed it for you."

"B-But you . . ." I stammered. "You're in jail . . . I mean . . . How did you get here?"

"Let's get out of the light." He turned and marched to a nearby pine tree.

I followed him, keeping my distance. His Winchester leaned against the tree trunk, the steel barrel glinting in the moonlight. "Why do you have the rifle?"

"Problems might come up."

"Roberto has Brad's rifle," I blurted.

"I'm not surprised."

"You're not?"

"No. He threatened to take it every time Brad went hunting. I guess the eagle was too much for him."

"Yeah," I said. "I guess so."

I forced myself to look up at him. "Why are you here? Did they drop your case?"

"No." He grabbed the rifle. "Karen came down and gave the prosecutor an earful. They're going to fry me, Megan."

I stared hard at him. "Don't say that."

He shook the rifle. "I won't go back. That cell

smells like sewage and looks worse."

"How did you get out? Are the police after you?"

"It's a long story."

"But—"

He held up a hand to silence me.

"Darren, you can't run away." It sounded so lame. "I'll find out the truth about Brad. I will."

"Just let me handle it, Megan—alone." He jammed the rifle butt into the ground.

"Why?"

"Remember when I said I hoped you didn't regret helping me?"

"Yes," I said softly.

"Well, you regret it, don't you?"

I paused one second too long. "No."

"You don't lie, remember?"

"I'm not lying. It's hard to explain. I can't be sorry I helped you, and I can't be glad I helped you. Not until I know all the answers."

He smiled sadly. "Curiosity killed the cat."

"That's not what killed Taffy. And it won't kill me." I gave him what I hoped was a determined look. "What are you going to do now?"

He glanced down at the rifle. "I know how to keep Karen from lying about me in court."

I clutched his arm. "Don't do anything that'll get you into more trouble. Promise me!"

"You'd better take the canoe and get back before your brother calls out the FBI." The rifle shone in the moonlight as he strode to the canoe, dragged the boat from the bushes, and slid the hull over the sand into the water.

"Don't worry about it," I said. "He doesn't notice anything lately."

"Get going, Megan."

I backed into the water. "Did you build a fire in the clearing tonight?"

"I was up there, yeah."

"Did you see anything weird?"

He frowned and looked away. "No."

He was lying.

"What about that awful screech I heard a while ago?"

"A coyote."

"It didn't sound like a coyote to me."

"So now you're a wildlife expert?"

I shoved my hands into the pockets of my sweatshirt. "How did you get here without the Bayliner, Darren?"

"Don't you ever run out of questions? I don't have time for this." He spat the words at me, then turned and marched down the beach.

"Darren, wait! Should I come back tomorrow? Do you need food?"

He walked slowly back to me, and when he spoke his voice was softer. "I won't be here."

"Where are you going?"

"Someplace that'll get me out of this mess." He grabbed the canoe and steadied it. "Here you go."

"Where?" I demanded. "Mexico? Canada?"

He just shook his head.

I climbed in and picked up the paddles. I looked at him and opened my mouth to say something more, but he quickly shoved the boat into the water, grabbed the rifle, and headed up the path to the clearing, a dark figure disappearing into the night.

Chapter 14

Apprehension hung in the air like the scent of skunk, as the five of us set out from the lodge for our hike up Devil's Tail Peak the next morning.

I'd gone back to the lodge the night before feeling frustrated. Things hadn't turned out at all like I'd hoped. Julie hadn't been on the island, and if I was going to find out anything from her, there was no choice but to climb this ugly mountain. Lack of sleep made me lightheaded, and I knew it would get worse as we climbed higher. No trail materialized to guide us up the sheer granite wall. From the start, we were too busy hiking to talk. The packs we carried made it grindingly hard work.

Karen led the group, with Roberto at her heels, his hair in a braid tied with a strip of leather. Behind them, Julie and James stuck together like moss on a rock. I brought up the rear. Karen wasn't making allowances for anybody. Even James had to focus all his energy on the granite slabs and grassy pockets ahead of us.

Where was Darren now? I wondered. On his way out of the country?

Karen wouldn't give us a break, and the

morning passed with the sun glaring off the mountain, sucking out our energy. Around noon I heard a noise that sounded like thunder. We rounded a ledge to find a waterfall spilling icy water from the cliff above us. We ripped off our socks and boots and jumped into the pool at the bottom of the falls, yelling and splashing each other. For a moment, things seemed almost normal, and we collapsed by the rushing water to eat our sandwiches, guzzle water from our water bottles, and get our energy back. At this altitude, even the wildflowers looked dizzy, holding on to the earth for their fragile little lives.

There was no time to laze around if we wanted to make the summit before dark, and we'd hardly swallowed the last of our sandwiches when Karen urged us to our feet. She led us around overhanging boulders and spears of rock. As the air thinned, the temperature dropped. My lungs ached from the effort of breathing the thin air. Soon, my leg muscles began to cramp, and it became torture just to put one foot in front of the other.

"We're more than halfway there. We should make the peak by sunset," Karen yelled at one point in the afternoon.

I can't make it, I thought. This was the craziest thing I'd ever done. By the time we got to the top, everyone would be too wiped out to open their mouths, much less reveal some big truth about murder. But when I thought of Darren, I had to keep going.

After a while, I developed a rhythm. Step, lunge, dig in. Step, lunge, dig in. The mountain loomed high, but I could see blue sky at the top. We were getting there.

Suddenly I couldn't make a wrong move. I was a mountain goat, a bighorn sheep, prancing up the sheer rock. I got this feeling sometimes when I surfed. I'd catch a big wave and ride it forever, as if I were part of the sea. I didn't have to think out the moves. The ocean and I just flowed together. The one thing I knew not to do was look down. The feeling of hands on my shoulders—hands that meant to kill me—still haunted me from my dream.

Directly ahead, Julie's pale hair floated around her shoulders. Her thin legs scrambled up the wall of granite. She said something to James, and he frowned and moved ahead. I caught up to her, and she turned to me. Her sweet smell made my stomach sway.

"Darren's free, isn't he, Megan?" Her amber eyes were open wide.

I tried not to show the shock I felt. "What do you mean?"

She smiled. "He's out of jail."

I looked at her.

"And he's here."

"Here?" I said dumbly.

"I feel his negative energy."

"Is he the one? The one you said was dangerous?"

She shook her head. "I don't know. Too many

confusing signs. Something covers the truth. But that person is here. On the mountain."

I looked around as if I expected to see my enemy pop out from behind a rock. The others were moving ahead quickly. "Were you on the island last night?"

"No. James and I had dinner at my house. We decided to go to bed early because of the hike today."

I stared closely at her. Was she telling me the truth? "Why are you after my brother?"

"I told you. He needs me. To teach him how to use his divine power."

"Give me a break," I snorted. "James can be a total geek sometimes, but I've never seen him act selfish until he met you. He used to care about people."

"He needs to care more for himself."

"He's dropping out of the university. Do you think that's caring for himself?"

"He was going to school for the wrong reasons."

"I think you're full of it," I said.

Julie smiled. "James will make his own choices, Megan. That is how it should be."

She was right about that. A lot of what Julie said was true. But how had she known Brad would die?

Her eyes were nearly as light as the yellow wildflowers that grew by the stream. "Don't worry, Megan. Tonight the crystals will reveal the truth. We will know everything."

I moved quickly away from her.

*   *   *

The afternoon rolled away like the face of the mountain, and by sunset, our weary group arrived at the tip of the Devil's Tail.

"Over here, hikers." Karen beckoned us to the eastern slope, and I gasped as we looked down. The cliff plunged thousands of feet to the valley below.

I moved away from the others and looked out as the sun burned the sky with crimson rays. A primitive world of towering mountains surrounded me, more awesome than anything I'd ever seen. The quiet caught and held me, and I felt that God must be close by. I barely moved for a long time, drinking in the beauty and power of the majestic peaks.

As I gazed out at the scenery, hands clamped down on my shoulders. I started and spun around. "Karen!"

"A little jumpy?"

I stared at her. "You surprised me is all."

She smiled. "Just wanted to point out the lodge down there. You can barely make out the roof. See? Over there between the two pines? And there's Desolation Valley. Remember where we left the trail? Keep going into the valley, and you'll catch all the trout you can eat."

"I see." I backed away from the edge. "Think I'll walk around a little."

I climbed around several clumps of rock and a mangled-looking juniper to find Roberto standing by himself, looking down from the cliff.

"Where did the men fall?" I asked him quietly.

He pointed. "See that narrow ledge, about ten yards down?"

"They were walking along *there*?"

He shook his head. "Craziness. Pure craziness."

Suddenly there was a sweet scent in the air. I turned. Julie stood a few feet away. "It won't be long now, Megan. Be patient." Her eyes glowed like a cat's in the shadow of the boulders behind us. Dirt smudged her left cheek.

"I need to find out what happened to Brad," I said.

She smiled. "I know."

Roberto snorted and nearly bumped into James as he walked away. My brother sauntered over and put one arm around Julie and one around me. "I'll bet you women are getting hungry. You did some heavy-duty climbing today. Meg, I'm proud of you."

"Thanks," I said.

"Come on, you slackers." Karen's voice carried over the rocks. "Let's get the fire started over here."

We built the fire next to a sheer wall of rock. The moon rose, gold and round, over the mountains. It felt as though our little group were hanging suspended in the night sky.

"Ready to do your thing, Julie?" Karen unrolled her sleeping bag and shook it out, then sat cross-legged on the padding. We all did the same.

Julie dumped the crystals, and something made the fire flare up. I thought I felt a strange presence. I glanced quickly at James, but he seemed lost in his own thoughts. I stayed quiet, waiting.

The crystals flashed their bright lights, burning like small fires. Julie moved the stones back and forth over the cloth, studying their formations.

"Is there room for one more at this party?" The angry voice brought our heads up as if there had been a shot.

Darren stood by a pile of boulders, his rifle tightly clutched in his fist. For a second, no one moved or spoke. A smile came to my lips. You didn't run away, after all, I thought. You're here, on the mountain, like Julie said.

And then my smile turned to a quick stab of fear as he lunged toward Karen.

Chapter 15

*K*aren leaped to her feet and scrambled away from Darren, putting out her hands as if to protect herself from a blow. "How did you get out of jail?" she demanded.

His lip lifted in the familiar crooked smile. "Believe it or not, my lawyer got me out—my *new* lawyer."

"Sam Hargrove!" I said, smiling broadly.

"Right." He shot me a smile in return. "Mr. Hargrove got my bail reinstated and called my parents. They came back and told the judge they'd make sure I didn't jump bail again."

"Figures," Karen said.

"Does it?" He took another step toward her. Now they were only inches apart. "Then figure on this, Karen. You're not going to tell any more lies about me. I'm never going back to jail."

Karen glared at him. "You don't have a choice, unless you plan to kill me in front of four witnesses."

"Kill *you*?" He laughed harshly.

All of us were on our feet now. James stepped forward, and I grabbed his arm. "Stay out of it," I said quietly.

"Hold this for me, will you?" Darren held out the rifle to James, who took it and nodded.

Then Darren pulled a white envelope from his jacket pocket. "I won't have to go back because I've got these!" A photograph fell to the ground. I moved quickly and scooped it up in my hand. It was one of the photographs we'd gotten from Ron Yarrow. The picture was ugly. Corpses marked with wounds stared up from the ground with blank eyes.

"Are you crazy?" Karen screamed. "Bringing these pictures up here? You know Father died on this mountain. You're even more sadistic than I thought."

"Lay off her, Darren." Roberto moved to put his arm around Karen.

"Don't be a fool, Roberto." Darren walked around our little circle, passing out photos to each one of us. "Look closely, everyone. Look at Stefan's arm, and tell me what you see."

I stared hard at the photograph in my hand, my eyes going over every centimeter of it. Then, suddenly, I felt the breath leave my body. "No wonder Brad freaked out when he saw these," I whispered.

"What is it?" James asked.

"Right there." I pointed to a spot on the print. "On the inside of Stefan's wrist. It's Karen's shield carved into his skin. It's not very obvious with all the other scratches and cuts on him, but when you look carefully . . . Brad would have known immediately." I looked up. Karen was scowling at me.

"It's the mark you make on all your kills," said Roberto to Karen, his dark eyes filling up with tears as he looked at her.

"You just couldn't resist, could you, Karen," said Darren, shaking his head. He folded his arms and took a deep breath. "My lawyer is going to the police to ask to have the bodies exhumed. I think the medical examiner might also find wounds made by arrows. Your arrows!"

Karen stared defiantly at us. "You're crazy," she said. She grabbed the packet of remaining pictures from Darren's hand and heaved it into the fire. The flames sizzled around them as she snatched the photographs from each of our hands to add to the flames. "Give me those."

"There's another set," I said.

"In case you're thinking of burning your arrows, too, I've already stopped by the storage shed and picked up a handful," Darren said.

"You took my arrows?" she screamed.

Darren closed his eyes tightly, as if he were in pain. When he spoke, his voice was soft. "I was so desperate sitting in that cell that I actually prayed that Brad would speak to me from the grave," he said. "Let me know what really happened."

Karen snorted. "You're even crazier than I thought."

"Go on," James urged him.

Darren's eyes opened, shining with tears. "Thanks to Megan, Sam Hargrove decided to represent me. After I was let out of jail, he insisted that my parents and I meet in his office.

At one point, he took my parents into his kitchen for coffee. That's when I saw it—a file he'd kept on Brad's telephone call to him."

"Phone call? What phone call?" Karen stood to her full height, arms folded. Her voice sounded shrill.

"He couldn't tell you about his conversation with Brad because of lawyer-client privilege," James said. "So he left his notes on it where you would find them."

"That's my take on it," Darren replied.

Darren turned back to Karen. "Brad called Mr. Hargrove the day before he died. You know why he did that, Karen? To ask the lawyer to help *you* out. He said that you had shot his father and yours with arrows, causing them to fall to their deaths."

"Oh, Karen," Julie said.

Roberto backed away from her. "You were up on the mountain that day, Karen," he said. "I'd climbed to the falls that afternoon and saw you hiking down. I called out to you, but you didn't hear me. You just kept going. When I asked you later, you said you'd been hunting at Desolation."

"And I saw you heading up the mountain that morning," Julie said. "I was awake before dawn. Something woke me—it must have been the crystals—and I went to the window. But I never connected seeing you with your father's death. That must be what the crystals have been trying to tell me."

"The truth was there all the time, " said Darren, "just like Megan said."

"Come on, Karen, admit it," I demanded. "Admit what you did!"

"Murderers have been convicted on less evidence," James said. "And once the autopsy results come back . . . Well, Karen, you might as well tell the truth."

Karen walked to the cliff and looked down into dark space. She stood there for a long time. We waited, hardly daring to breathe.

She turned to face us. "All right! I guess you'll find out soon enough. Yes, I shot them. They deserved it! I did it for Brad and me. We wanted to start our lives together, but our fathers wouldn't give us the money we needed. I followed Father up the mountain that day to show him how well I'd mastered everything he'd taught me. I was a better climber and a better archer than him or any of his precious royal relatives. I was a true Valkyrie!"

"Poor Karen," Roberto said. "You've always had to prove yourself to your dad."

"For a while, I watched them climb. They didn't see me. I was about to tell them I was there when I saw them go up on that ledge. Suddenly it struck me how easy it would be to get them to lose their balance—just brush them back with my arrows, and down they'd go. I'd collect the arrows and there would be no evidence of what I'd done. Then Brad and I would have everything we wanted, with no waiting. But my hands must have been shaking, because my aim was off. The arrows hit them, instead of just grazing them."

She continued to speak, the defiance in her voice growing. "I thought Brad hated his dad as much as I hated mine and would be glad he was dead, but he wasn't. And after a while he began to suspect that I'd been involved. Maybe I seemed too calm after the deaths. After he saw the photographs, he confronted me, and I told him the truth. He said I was crazy, that he couldn't love me anymore. What a wimp he turned out to be!"

"You killed Brad, too, didn't you?" I asked softly.

Karen's eyes narrowed as she looked off into the star-studded sky. "He threatened to tell. He wanted me to go with him to a lawyer. I told him he was nuts. He didn't tell me that he'd already spoken to one! He also said he was leaving Sapphire Lake, to go to Hollywood. He wanted to see if he could get more acting jobs. All our plans were in ruins—thanks to *him*!"

Karen lunged toward Darren, her face suddenly contorted with rage. Roberto grabbed her arms and held her back.

"It's all *your* fault, for getting him that movie job!" she screamed at Darren. Her eyes shot angry sparks as she turned to face the rest of us. "He betrayed me. Can't you see that? He betrayed me!"

Darren took a step toward her. "You set my boat engine to blow up. You watched us on location and learned how to use explosives. Were you trying to kill me, too?" Darren asked.

She waved him off. "I didn't care if you died in

the explosion. You were always taking Brad away from me."

"And when Darren wasn't killed, you figured he would get blamed for Brad's murder," I said.

She shrugged. "That's right." Her bitter words poisoned the night air.

"Then Megan came along and started stirring things up," James said.

"Yeah." She glared at me. "Miss Nosy couldn't leave things alone. When Julie's warnings didn't work, I tried to scare her off with a rifle shot."

"I thought you were on a fishing trip that morning!" I said in shock.

"The people I told you I had taken fishing had checked out already, so they couldn't blab the truth."

"My warnings were to *help* Megan, not hurt her," Julie interjected, looking dazed. "You really killed Brad?"

Karen reached toward her, but Julie shrank back from the other girl's hand.

"I couldn't let him leave me, could I, Julie?" Karen begged. "You always told me to draw on my inner power, to use it to make things turn out the way I wanted. And it worked. You gave me the strength to get rid of Father. If anybody deserved to die, he did! And to keep Brad here with me, forever, at Sapphire Lake."

Julie backed away from her in horror. "But I didn't mean . . . You can't blame me for their deaths."

"*I* do," Roberto yelled. "I blame you in spades."

Julie's body went slack, and for a second I thought she was going to faint. Her hands opened, and the crystals spilled to the ground.

I turned to Karen. "You pushed me, didn't you? When I was here years ago. The water was below us. I was so scared."

She snorted. "You thought you were so great, always outrunning and outswimming me. I had to show Father you weren't brave, like me. But he yelled up at me to stop, even though he'd pushed me off that same ledge more than once."

I remembered now. Looking down, I'd seen Mr. Thorsten's angry face as he'd yelled up at Karen. And then I'd seen Darren right behind him, and I'd called out his name. My dream was clear now. Karen was messed up even then. Stefan had done that. And Darren was innocent.

I reached out and touched Darren's arm. I was glad to see the scowl melt from his face as he looked at me. "It's over," I said. "You're finally free."

Chapter *16*

The Bayliner rocked gently next to the lodge dock as Darren and I sat on the leather seat, soaking up the sun and sharing his field glasses.

"You don't have much experience as a birder, do you?" He handed me the binoculars.

I aimed the glasses at the top of the island. "Well, how was I supposed to know it was an eagle that night on the island? I've never heard one in my life, or seen one, either. You could have explained."

"I couldn't believe it was back myself. I guess I was afraid to believe. It was just about to touch down. Then it spotted you and screamed in terror." He laughed. It sounded good to hear him happy.

It had been three days since the night on Devil's Tail Peak. No one slept that night, and the climb down the next day was quiet and tense. But Karen hadn't made any trouble. She said she knew she'd get off after what her father had done to her. And James agreed that she could plead insanity and make a good case.

I looked at Darren. He could have easily been in the boat when it exploded. The scars didn't seem so bad when I thought about how close he'd come to getting killed.

I raised the binoculars to my eyes. "I don't think I'll ever see an eagle."

Wait! Was that a flash of wing? No, only a rock reflecting the sun.

Darren touched my shoulder. "James is yelling for you. He's on the porch."

"I know. I can't believe it, but he finally admitted I was right about something. He's going back to the university. He's his old bossy self again. Just ignore him. That's what I do."

"Well, it's good to have him as a friend again." Darren looked up at the lodge.

"Did Karen's mom go back to the police station this morning?" he asked.

"Yes. Roberto went with her for moral support. They're meeting Karen and her lawyer there. I promised I'd help out at the lodge while they're gone." I sent a dismissive wave toward the porch. "Julie's helping, too. She and James can handle things for a while."

Darren smiled as James disappeared into the lodge.

"What are you thinking about?" I asked.

"Julie's face when Roberto accused her of meddling in things she didn't understand." He laughed. "It was awesome the way he told Julie off."

"Yeah." I smiled. "I don't think Julie meant to hurt anybody, though."

"Maybe not, but she sure gave Karen ideas."

"And James, too. My dad was right. The occult world can suck you in and chew you up. And I never thought I'd say this, but I'm glad James is his old self again." I lowered the binoculars and looked at Darren. "Can you ever forgive Karen for killing Brad and then trying to frame you?"

"I don't know."

I sighed. "What about the others? Can you forgive them? They all believed you killed Brad."

"You didn't." His dark blue eyes shone with a light I hadn't seen before.

"You're right," I said. "I knew you couldn't murder anyone. I felt it in my heart, even if my mind was a little confused."

"I don't blame the others for thinking I was guilty," Darren said. "I gave them reasons. I'm free now. That's all that counts." He smiled. "And the eagles are back."

"I wish I could see one." I reached for the binoculars.

"Megan."

I lowered the glasses to my lap.

"I couldn't have made it without you," he said. "I acted like a real jerk a few times. Even before Brad died, I . . . well, I've been a jerk more than once. I guess it's because I didn't have a friend who really cared about me. Thanks for being there."

I looked hard at him. "You never did tell me why you hit Brad."

"He told me about going to Hollywood. He said he was going to leave without telling Karen.

It seemed so cowardly. If only I'd known why he was leaving without telling her. Maybe if I'd listened better—been a better friend—I could have saved his life."

"You can't blame yourself," I said. "Brad made a terrible mistake by not telling the police what he knew right away."

"Yeah," Darren said. "You know, I hold Stefan responsible for all this more than Karen. His abuse really messed her up."

"Why didn't anyone stop him? Didn't Mrs. Thorsten know about it?"

"Stefan could be very charming. The few times we saw him get on Karen's case, we figured he was being a jerk but that it was none of our business. As for Karen's mom, maybe she didn't want to see what was going on."

I nodded. "Did you suspect Karen all along?"

"No, not really. But when I saw the file in Sam Hargrove's office, I realized Brad had called the lawyer to talk about *Karen*, not himself. I wondered how Brad could know about the murders, and then I remembered the photos. I figured he must have seen something in them, so I studied them hard. Finally I spotted Karen's mark on her father. Then it all clicked in my brain."

"Suddenly you could understand why Karen might want to kill Brad, and why Brad might be trying to get away from her."

Darren nodded. "Carving that shield on her father was a really sick, barbaric act. Brad's betrayal must have put her over the edge, and she decided to kill him, too."

He sighed. "I guess I could have waited for the autopsies and the police to examine the evidence, but I figured that if I could confront Karen on the mountain, she might break down and confess in front of everyone."

"Why didn't you tell me what you'd found out that night when we saw each other on the island?"

"I wanted to be the one to confront Karen, and to do it in my own way. For Brad. Do you understand?"

I looked at him for a moment. "Yes, I think so."

I raised the binoculars to my eyes. "I don't think I'll ever see an eagle."

I felt him tip the binoculars up until they focused on the highest peak of the island. "Just look beyond the obvious, Megan. To the places most people never look."

"I'm good at that."

"I know you are," he said softly.

And then I saw them. Giant wings lifting into the sky.